Quall Assassin

Talaza's Contract

Talaza Bane is an assassin. His next target is now identified.
To his employer he is an instrument.

Sometimes instruments rebel.

Novella 5

Yuan Jur

Cover art : Ralph Manis/Infinitee Designs

Australia

Quall Assassin by Yuan Jur

ISBN-13: 978-0-9942153-6-9 (Paperback)

ISBN-13: 978-0-9942153-9-0 (E-Book Epub)

ISBN-13: 978-0-9942153-8-3 (E-Book MOBI)

Cover and art design by Ralph Hawke Manis of Infinitee Designs 2017

www.infinitee-designs.com

Book design and production by WaaDoom in association with

Thebookpatch.com

Editing and structure by Charles Wannop and De Chao Peterson

Dedication

To the dedicated Citadel 7 crew, the backers LMA, Copy Editor JDK, Cover artist "Ralph the Brush" Manis, production manager CW, promotion LA and beta testers NC, DW & Co, thank you. These are the people no one hears about. You all continue to be awesome. Thanks for helping the Citadel 7 fans Enter The Superverse.

Finally, a special dedication to our amazing and inspirational structure editor, Mary Rosenblum, who tragically passed in the early months of 2018. Thank you Mary, your guidance and confidence in our series will be carried in our hearts always.

Orders

"Welcome, Agent. This mission propels us along the Superverse Continuum through the endless oceans of Dark Matter. We will emerge in a timeline where some things will seem familiar, others quite strange. The voice of Central will now take you through our brief. See you on the ground. Mission success to us all!"

C-DATE: CLASSIFIED.

UNFOLDING TIMELINE: ACTIVE.

MISSION AUTHORIZATION: EVERCYCLE SEVEN.

MISSION POINT OF ORIGIN: TORAN STAR SYSTEM, PLANET TORA.

PLANET SECURITY LEVEL: 10.

LOCAL TIME: CLASSIFIED.

LOCATION: LUDD CONTINENT.

MISSION CATALYST: DETECTION OF RIFT IN NATURAL KARMA STREAM.

CONSCRIPTION OF INDIGENOUS MORTALS: APPROVED

Act 1

CHAPTER

1

Tasked with Trouble

It is late afternoon during the season of leaf-fall. A storm is in the distance. Bitter cold wind and the onset of rain have begun battering the terrain across the continent of Ludd. A member of Black Mountain's Quall Assassin Cosa Clan, Talaza, stands on a lonely outcrop in deep thought. He is looking to the border east. He knows his mountain can be seen from distant leagues by many of his clan's employers. Staring away to the far horizon, he contemplates recent turbulent events. He is alone, as always, speaking his thoughts aloud:

"I am Talaza Bane. Enemies and allies call our world 'Tora.' It means 'engage.' Our land is Ludd's heart. This is where the heavens turned Quall from light to solid and our purpose was defined by the voice on the wind who spoke to our first mystic, Korta.

"The deep ocean waters lay many days' walk through dangerous forest and ribbon grasses of the rolling tundra away to east Ludd's shores. Our Cosa Clan and mystics are oldest of all Quall clans and have far reach and respect even amidst those with only two arms and legs. We Quall of Black Mountain are highest prized in the Quall Assassin Guild of greater Ludd for our stealth, use of blade, and secret ways of removing our patron's targets. There are many Kurja —those with open face—who need a Quall's skill to remove what they cannot. Other clans not Quall are known to us beyond the shadow of Black Mountain. Our mountain's heart has not shaken since my youth when my face was covered from sunlight. Elder Makayass says Black Mountain is pleased with our clan's determination to fulfill our purpose before we are returned to dust. We Quall of Black Mountain in turn respect the life and sanctuary our mountain provides.

"As I stand on this red cliff looking down on the stendle tree valley below, with only my thoughts to listen to, the winds have changed and grown cold for another round. Leaf-fall is at hand. Soon the water-silk will begin to drop, covering the earth in white. In rounds past, Quall of Black Mountain would not leave until the season of bloom begins. But since Mystic Tatute told Elder Makayass of seeing the Star Lord descend in the west valley, I know this time will be different."

A lull in the wind allowed his keen hearing to pick up the steps of someone on approach. He looked over his shoulder to see the familiar slender form of his wife, Analuke, moving toward him.

"Talaza?" she called. "Talaza! Oh, there you are. Thought I might find you here on your ledge. Arguing in your head again?"

Talaza harrumphed as his wife closed the distance and stopped behind him just beyond arms' reach. He folded both sets of his arms and turned to look back to the horizon.

"My bones are uneasy, Analuke. We have been wed long enough for you to know my bones don't lie. I know our mountain will see great change very soon."

Though he wasn't looking at her, Talaza knew Analuke was rolling her eyes, as she always did when he spoke like this.

"You could at least turn around to talk to me, husband. Your eyes always tell to me the deeper meanings before your words caress my ears. Talaza, please."

Reluctantly, Talaza turned to face her.

She nodded. "That's better. Oh, but look at you . . . Fingers twitching on all four hands! And you look like you've forgotten how to wrap your head." Her eyes sparkled with mischief, betraying the smile that surely played on her lips beneath her own head wraps. "What example is this for our sons?"

"My concerns are for all our future with what we've seen." He let the two arms covering his lower ribs fall by his side and then dropped his eye line for a moment. "Nervous? Yes, of course I am, wife! You saw it too, up close."

Analuke sighed. "Husband, you were supposed to be tutoring Sooza in blade craft an hour ago. His rite of passage is coming soon; he's depending on you. What has you so picked apart? We presented our findings and there is an end to it."

"Analuke . . . when Makayass ordered us to investigate the place Tatute spoke of and bring back what our eyes beheld, I thought it would be something quite different. What we had to tell caused much whisper between Mystic Tatute and Elder Makayass."

"So? They always do a lot of whispering."

Talaza shook his head. "Not like this time. This was different. When that falling star slowed and settled in the forest below, it really stirred them up. There is a deeper meaning, Analuke. The Star Lords are planning something. They are in league with the wind's voice—I know it."

"Husband, Elder Makayass has been to consult Mystic Tatute many times as the moons have crossed our sky this round."

"Yes, wife of mine, but Elder Makayass sent messengers to the other clans this time and then called for the Great Circle to convene. Not in half my lifetime has he done that. That was two nights ago. And we are also on the eve of a master-level elimination. It is not a good sign."

"We all heard Mystic Tatute, under the sign of both half-moons and in front of all the clan elders of the four directions. Yes, he told of a great change coming to our world. But it was the *stranger* he seemed more concerned about than the Star Lords. He said it is the stranger we must prepare for. The stranger is the one who will bring the change. We are but soldiers who have our place. Elder Makayass points us and we eliminate the target. That's all we need to concern ourselves with, husband. If that target be the stranger, then we shall see the order filled and then move on."

Talaza began to pace slowly back and forth. "Mystic Tatute said he heard the Dark Star's voice on the wind again this morning, wife. This always means an omen of twisted things. And twisted things never favor the Quall in the long run. I have seen it."

"So my husband is now a mystic too?"

"Stop straining your top-knot, wife. You know what I meant! Tatute is never wrong."

"Well, you best come see what else he has to say, then. The bones have chosen you and me to leave the mountain. We must see to a problem involving a Scarzen captain and one of the Flaxon regent's high officials from Weirawind. Does *that* sound like something to better occupy your time?"

Talaza nodded.

"Come on," Analuke said. "We have been summoned."

∗∗∗

At the center of Black Mountain hamlet stood Elder Makayass's wood-and-stone Yurt of Parley. Talaza and Analuke entered. Inside they smelled the scent of fragrant leaves burning amongst the ashes of the in-ground fire pit in the yurt's center. While sparse in its furnishing, the space was welcoming, with rugs strewn at different strategic places for guests of different status. Talaza watched smoke spiral aloft in ribbons to dissipate through a conical cover sealing the roof. He unclasped his hamlet plaid. Analuke, two paces behind, did the same with her arisaid. Both folded their shoulder garment displaying their clan colors into the customary triangle shape. They then moved toward the interview rugs near the feet of Elder Makayass. Mystic Tatute, scrawny in build even for a Quall, stood to Makayass's left. His thin-fingered black-gloved hands pressed over the pommel of his divining spear that stood level to his sternum.

Tall for a Quall at five feet two inches, Makayass sat on a robust U-shaped stendle-wood throne. The skin of a majestic Great Mountain Bearcat adorned the backrest. The head of the predator sat mounted on a hidden frame at his right shoulder. Its open jaws exposed the creature's double rows of back angled teeth that had been rumored to have left their mark on Makayass. This was the carnivore that he had killed to earn his rite of passage as clan leader. The bearcat skin's tan-and-black striped coloring sat in contrast against the black-and-crimson bindings covering Makayass from head to knee. His indigo blue torso overgarment remained partially obscured by his body-length golden brown Elken skin apron of office.

Makayass gestured for the two arrivals to sit. Complying, they sat side by side after pressing the palms of their top two hands together in respectful salute. Their leader looked to the entrance and dismissed the two gray-clad assassins concealed in shadow on either side of the door. He leaned forward, resting one elbow on an arm rail of his throne.

"Your observations have caused quite a stir," Makayass said.

Talaza glanced at Analuke. "Told you," he said under his breath.

"You have both been chosen for a task of great importance," said Makayass. "A task where a Quall's skill will be tested to the highest level."

Makayass shot Tatute a glance before continuing, "Mystic Tatute has foreseen a fork in the road of the destiny for all who occupy Ludd."

Tatute stepped forward, his cutting stare bent first on Talaza and then Analuke. He raised his divining spear speaking in an aged cracked tone. "Hear my words, Blades of this clan. The dawn of a new way approaches and brings chaos and much unnecessary loss of life. The Dark Star, Hex, has spoken to

Tatute on the wind and in dream. The bones confirm his words. A stranger, one who is not natural to this world, is coming. We must alter the course of his influence. An opportunity has arisen."

"Yes," Makayass cut in. "I have received word from the Chou king, Wang So Tan, of a clandestine meeting between the Scarzen of Talon East and the Flaxon of Weirawind City. It will take place in two turns of the sun in the mid night of the second day. They meet at the mouth of Yorr Pass, in the Neutral Zone."

Talaza and Analuke glanced at each other.

Makayass went on, "Three is the number reported to attend for each clan and involves a parley about the expansion of the Neutral Zone. Wang So Tan, our present patron, has sent each a forged invitation. He has also issued a strike order on the leader of each clan's delegation. He requests the placing of incriminating evidence on each target, blaming the other for the strike. Talaza shall strike the Flaxon target, you, Analuke, shall deal with the Scarzen commander."

Talaza passed another glance Analuke's way.

"Your eyes express quandary, Talaza," Makayass said.

Talaza went to speak, but Analuke's words pushed forward first: "Great Makayass. The Scarzen and the Flaxon have been at knife point since Quall were transformed from light. Anyone who knows the two clans would find such negotiations to their mutual benefit . . . umm—suspicious. Chou are devious in their dealings, known often for abandoning an ally to save their own neck. Remember what happened to Menengus four seasons ago?"

Makayass nodded.

"Then I ask you: why would the Scarzen sympathize with anything the Flaxon have to say? The only way they have spoken for generations is with sharp blades and much death. I believe that Wang So Tan's true target is the

Quall. I think there is no meeting. I think he intends to lay blame on us. Quall ore makes blade metal second only to that of the Scarzen. He has failed in previous negotiations for the ore our mountain contains. Why not get others to obliterate the Quall while he moves in from our northern border to claim the spoils?"

"Menengus was your brother, Analuke," said Makayass. "I understand your pain. Should that be the case, then Quall law applies and Wong So Tan himself shall become the prime target of every Quall."

"I think this all centers on what we saw in the valley," Talaza said. "I think it has to do with the Star Lord's recent coming and going. Perhaps they have made a pact."

Talaza noticed Tatute gently shake his head.

"The Star Lord's coming and this meeting, the bones say are separate," Tatute said.

"Chou and Flaxon borders have always been in contention," Makayass said. "We should not look for higher purpose when old scores are plainly being settled. The Chou gain their wealth from digging in the ground. Their tunnels are running dry of ore. Flaxon land will offer them new beginnings. They also covet the mountains where the Scarzen dwell. Spies tell me they seek access to the blue spirit crystal that the Scarzen guard within."

"Their ambition will see their annihilation should they draw Scarzen attentions in such matters," Talaza said.

Makayass nodded. "Chou clan numbers are swelling. They are simply running out of room. The fertile fields the Flaxon use to grow their crops are of great interest to the Chou to feed their masses. All Kurja are not so different and covet each other's land. We Quall merely administer a balance from time to time."

"So you think the Chou want to start open war between the Scarzen and the Flaxon?" Analuke asked. "This means they intend to sift through the spoils afterward. They must have their head wrapped backwards if they can't see what result that will have."

"Wife, hold your opinion," Talaza said. "Forgive my wife, great Makayass. Her opinions are sometimes . . . hard on wiser ears."

"Great Makayass," Analuke pressed. "The Scarzen are small in number by comparison to the other clans. Yet none have breached their bunker walls or broken them in open combat and returned the victor, not in the entire spoken history of the Quall. Scarzen power on the battlefield would see the Flaxon ground to meat paste should the Scarzen leave their border. Why do the Chou want to stir up such hostility? And what is to stop the Chou sweeping south to *our* mountain to look for the ore they value so much?"

Makayass sat back, considering Analuke's comment. "Not our concern, Analuke, for now," he said, tossing a glance to Tatute. "We have been paid well in advance with clink for the service we provide. Gather your best blades and may Hex grant your strokes cut true. Leave neither witness nor trace of your actions. You both depart at the setting sun. Should you encounter the Star Lord, treat them with reverence should they make demands of you. We know not their reason for being here."

Tatute stepped forward, raising his divining spear. "If you pass from form to light during the course of events, may Hex carry you to the greenest hunting ground."

Both Talaza and Analuke stood and paid respect. Then, just for a moment out of the corner of his eye, Talaza thought he saw a tall figure standing in shadow in the far corner of the room. He focused in on that position, which made the others look too.

"Have you some concern, Blade Master?" Tatute asked.

Talaza's eyes crimped and he frowned upon seeing the space empty. He made no reply. A hand gently touched him on the upper arm.

"Talaza," Analuke said softly.

His attention brought back, Talaza turned to Makayass. "May I make a request of the clan elder?" Talaza asked.

"You may," Makayass said.

"Our sons, Sooza and Cezarn, are due for their rite of passage very soon. In the event I or my wife do not return, I ask that the house of Makayass show them sanctuary and guidance."

"You have the word of Makayass. It will be done."

"We shall not fail you, great Makayass," Talaza said.

He and Analuke paid respect again, then they turned and departed.

****

Makayass watched the two leave before turning to Tatute. "Are you sure they will fulfill their part?" Makayass asked. "Will they encounter the stranger?"

"The bones were unclear on that question," Tatute said. "In my dream Hex told me the road would be treacherous and outcomes unexpected."

Makayass sighed. "Hex forever speaks in riddles. What does that mean?"

"Hex sees this world from a different place, and his wisdom is too deep for even the great Korta to fathom. Out of chaos comes order, this Hex guarantees. What is certain is, Hex's power grows. His aim for our part in his greater plan is yet to be revealed."

CHAPTER

2

Nooses and Hangmen

Talaza and Analuke left the hamlet to descend the west face of Black Mountain. They took goods and chattels for the three-day turnaround of their mission in a side-slung knapsack. No longer in their domestic coverings, both Quall wore chameleon greens, which fitted close to their body. Top-knots were bound with black slaa thread, plaited tight, slick with the residue of poisonous forma nettle for use on enemies.

A pair of dark lacquered knife belts crisscrossed their chest and back, bristling with black Quall throwing blades. Each knife cluster included a combination of blade types for differing tasks and applications. Both had additional blades sheathed on each shoulder and forearm. Talaza carried two long knives across his back. Analuke carried a laminated Quall bow and a quiver of ten jade-green feathered arrows with deep-bite heads.

Silk rain blown in from the west pressed on them, and flakes of ice glistened against the silver scales woven into their garments. Sure steps kept their pace steady. Soon they were below the squall that hammered the mountain's shoulder. However, it took them till sunrise to reach the foot of the mountain, where rock and plant life looked very different.

Down here, no longer did the iron-colored stone and gray shale from above dominate the landscape. Instead, underfoot was a carpet of turquoise-colored moss covering the stone, with tiny orchids sprouting through the cracks. From here, an increased thickening of the forest limited their depth of view.

They slowed, more cautious, moving like blending shadows for no unwelcome eyes to see. Here rain fell light but steady, pattering through tree branches above. In the distance Talaza could hear the bubble and ripple of a stream that they both knew well.

"We'll follow the stream for a time," Talaza said. "Then we'll exit at the edge of the Yorr Forest by end of day's light, if we keep moving."

They kept to the plan, stopping once to eat in a sheltered place, and made the next marker of Yorr Forest's edge in good time. Inside the tree line, they moved swiftly to the part of the forest where trunks grew thicker and sails of mist formed, giving the surroundings an eerie feel.

"There is the mouth of Yorr Pass," Talaza said, pointing.

Analuke nodded. "Where Makayass said the meet would take place."

Somewhere in the mid-distance, the chilling howl of some ravenous predator carried on the wind. Then, through the trees, from all directions came the sound of a tormented victim. The cry for help in what sounded like the last moments of life sent a shiver through the bones of both Quall. They ducked in alongside the great bulk of a fallen mossy stendle trunk and instinctively engaged their skill of chameleon focus, a power innate to all Quall. After the tiniest moment a soft radiance passed over their skin and garments. They seamlessly blended with the colors of their close surroundings and remained absolutely still.

"What was that?" Analuke whispered with concerned. "That did not sound like common tongue to me."

"Nor any words of Scarzen or Flaxon my ears have encountered," Talaza said.

Analuke drew a blade from her forearm scabbard. A sail of mist pushed passed them, accompanied by a flutter of leaves from the wind overhead.

"It could have been a razorboar in season," Talaza said.

"Then someone just cut off both of his stones," Analuke said.

After some moments with no sound of anything heading their way, the two relaxed their chameleon focus.

Talaza looked at Analuke and said, "Scout for good vantage points south and from the mouth of the pass, ye ken?"

Analuke nodded.

"To my eye," he said, "I think it likely the meeting will take place in that small clearing surrounded by those fallen stendle to the left."

"What are you going to do?"

"I am going to scout a short distance into the pass. Might be a good place for traps. Should you sight either target, loose a bird-whistle arrow."

"Alright."

Talaza moved off, leaving Analuke to scout in the opposite direction.

CHAPTER

3

Yorr Pass

Yorr Pass outlined a natural convergence of two great land masses in the central region of Ludd. Its path, essentially an ancient riverbed, had long since lost most of its water to subterranean channels. The mountain to the west—called Trilix Di, meaning Great Earth—had a cloud-covered summit legendary for being all but unassailable. The mountain to the east—Trilix Tian, or Sky Crystal Mountain—was riddled with treacherous catacombs and bottomless sinkholes. Both earth titans had reputation for deadly landslides. The shadow-filled passage that lay between them, particularly in the time of leaf-fall, was notorious for taking lives. Travelers who ventured there often found the remains of those preceding them crushed under a fallen boulder or buried under a mound of shale.

Quall eyes were well suited to seeing by moonlight. Even so, by the time Talaza had picked his way some fifty yards inside the dark mouth of the pass, he had to tread carefully. The deeper shadows around the craggy ledges and vertical faces of either shoulder had his mind playing tricks.

By Hex's heart, this place carries the chill of the dead, he thought.

He felt his breastbones twinge as if responding to the feeling. He looked back to the mouth of the pass and wondered about Analuke for a moment. He'd left a marker for her at the mouth, should she need to follow his trail. Talaza's next step froze in place when he felt a touch on his shoulder. Talaza turned and lashed out with a well-practiced backhand of his long knife. He expected to feel the drag of flesh behind padded armor or armored skin. But there was nothing. He drew a breath to steady himself, checking for any signs of movement.

Some rubble fell from the cliff face above. Striking the ground with a crack and clatter, stone fragments fell all around his position. Talaza drew a throwing blade from the sheaths on his chest-belts with his three free hands.

"Show yourself, Kurja!" he snapped in common tongue. "I'll make it quick!"

Heavy silence filled the surroundings for a long moment, then: "Alright, we're comin' out," said a mature male voice from the shadows. "Just put your blades away. We don't want any trouble. We just want to talk, Blade Master."

Unsettled by the way they had identified him, Talaza's view swung left and right. The nonthreatening voice seemed to come from several directions at once. He relaxed his arms but sheathed no blades. From a position behind his left shoulder, he heard steps of different kinds approaching. Turning sharply, he adopted a battle-ready stance to see a tall traveler stepping toward him with a confident stride. A dog padded along beside the traveler at his right heel.

At first the individual looked much like a Flaxon officer to Talaza, but quickly that opinion changed when he stepped into better light. His long gray duster and broad-brimmed hat were cut nothing like that of the Flaxon military or common citizen. Talaza's view went next to the dog—a short, stout breed he'd seen somewhere in his travels before. A female, with a scruffy gray coat and a black patch over one eye. The tip of her right ear was missing too, he noticed. It was the animal's intelligent stare that held Talaza's focus most. There was a potency to it that made him feel as though the dog somehow saw straight through him.

"We're not your enemy," said the traveler. "Not from around here, if you take my meaning. Now if you'd just put your blades away, we can talk like civilized folk."

Talaza's jaw tightened. "You are with the Flaxon!"

He hurled two blades across the void, one at each target. As the blades closed to strike, a soft green shield of energy spread in front of both the traveler and the dog. Each blade struck at eye height and froze for a blink in the green field before falling with a clatter to the ground. Talaza's eyes widened in surprise as he prepared his next throw.

The traveler raised his hands in a placating manner. "Wait! My name's Uniss."

"A war mage in Flaxon employ, then!" Talaza said, hurling another blade at Uniss's head.

Again the green energy field obstructed the blade's path.

"No, we're not!" Uniss shouted. "Just hear me out."

Somehow his words stayed Talaza's hand, though he didn't know why.

"How do you wield such power?" Talaza asked, standing a little more at ease.

"I am not Flaxon," said Uniss. He looked down to his companion cringing with the thought of how far that last shout might have carried. He softened his next words to Talaza. "Look, I just used a defense common where we come from. We mean you no harm. Let me prove it."

Uniss pointed to the canine. "Haven't you noticed? I have a dog. Her name's actually 'Dogg,' as in D-O-G-G. Flaxon don't treat their canines kindly, nor use this breed. Look closely. You know it to be true. She is free of tether, and neither charges nor bears teeth of aggression toward you."

Dogg made a soft whimper and wagged her tail as if on cue.

Talaza gave no reply.

"We are from a world very far from here," Uniss lent forward. "From beyond the stars."

Now Talaza's eyes widened. *Hex's blessing! The Star Lord?*

"Where we come from, some call this form 'man,'" Uniss said, gesturing down his torso with one hand. He paused, raising a hand to his ear as though listening. "Thanks, Trev," he said to some unknown party. "See if you can track him."

"So," said Talaza. "You *are* the Star Lord we have seen in the valley?"

"Yes," said the dog, stepping forward before Uniss could reply.

Talaza froze, staring in disbelief at the dog. "You . . . talk?"

"Yes. And if you don't start trusting us and stop being so suspicious," Dogg went on, "we'll all be in a lot more trouble than we already are."

Unconsciously, Talaza dropped his long knife onto the ground. His arms fell to his sides and he relaxed.

Uniss looked down to his companion. "Thanks, Dogg," he said. "*Not* exactly the entrance we agreed on."

"You heard Trevor, Uniss," Dogg said. "We only have a few minutes."

Uniss looked to Talaza. "Just so ya know, there's an armed company of Flaxon coming up the pass from the north. They'll be here real soon."

Snapping a look to the north bend, Talaza said almost inaudibly, "A whole company? Makayass said there would be only three."

"Let me tell you a little story about the fellas you're about to play with," Uniss said. "In the north there is a great river. Do you know it?"

"The Churn," Talaza said.

"That's the one. That river is used by the Flaxon to irrigate their lands and supply water to the city of Weirawind, their capital."

"What of it?"

"About halfway along is a fork that sends water south and eventually to the Yorr Fields. There, on the banks of that natural waterway, grows a very rare orchid."

Talaza frowned. "A flower—so?"

"Yes, a flower," Uniss said. "But this flower doesn't grow anywhere else in Ludd. The Scarzen use this orchid as part of a very special compound to aid citizens in their culture. They mix it with a substance they call trilix, a blue crystal found in the mountains they mine."

Talaza gave a curt nod. "The Scarzen spirit crystal has been known to the Quall for generations."

A half-smile lifted one corner of Uniss's mouth. "Ah, but the blue crystal and the orchids combine to make a salve that protects and heals them. In very rare cases they've even used it on the occasional outsider. That ties in to what we are investigating. It's something that will affect your entire world."

Talaza tilted his head to one side, wondering what Uniss was getting at.

"Do you know of the struggle between the Scarzen and Flaxon over the flow of water through Yorr Fields?" Uniss asked.

"Yes, we are aware of it," said Talaza, nodding slightly this time.

"The growth of their prized orchids in that area is in decline."

"And?"

"When the Scarzen realized that the Flaxon damming the waterway caused levels south to fall so low, they quickly put two and two together. So they moved in, sending raiding parties to destroy the dams the Flaxon had constructed."

"Yes, that too we have witnessed," Talaza said.

"Then you will also know that it resulted in a war. The Flaxon thought the Scarzen were attempting to destroy their water supply and food chain for future conquest."

"Ahhh, two sides seeing, or being shown, the wrong thing," Talaza said.

Now Uniss nodded. "Good. Then we recognize the same manipulation."

Talaza's mind flashed back to the words Analuke had spoken to their clan leader. He focused his gaze on Uniss and said, "I and another have a mission involving some Flaxon and Scarzen meeting nearby—soon."

"We know." Uniss glanced down at Dogg and then continued, "That's part of the reason we're here. The Scarzen think the Flaxon know something about the value of the orchid and its relationship to their trilix. To them the Flaxon threaten their mandate to protect the blue crystal. That's reason enough for all-out war for the Scarzen."

"Agreed," Talaza said.

"We saw this flare up with some considerable loss of life awhile back," Dogg said.

"Right," Uniss said. "It stopped only a full round ago when the Flaxon finished building another dam northwest of Weirawind, farther downstream. The Chou see an advantage here to tip the balance in their direction by setting the Scarzen and the Flaxon against each other."

Talaza nodded. *Just as Analuke said.*

"And the Chou intend ruling all of Ludd, including Black Mountain. Have you heard whisper of this?" Uniss asked.

"Some news has reached our mountain, yes," Talaza said.

"They want the fight to continue while they gather strength," Uniss said.

"Agreed," said Dogg. "But they are being pushed by another who is manipulating circumstance from behind."

"Hmm," Talaza muttered.

Analuke was right all along, he thought.

"Quall are happy if Flaxon die," Talaza said. "The Flaxon regent is without honor. He cares not who has been hurt in the past. Scarzen are a difficult target—very dangerous—but honorable warriors. They always need good reason to attack."

"The Flaxon aren't our favorite either, Blade Master," Dogg said.

"But we can't afford for them and the Scarzen to begin a larger war," Uniss said. "At least until we finish what we came to do. All this conflict is being fueled by something far darker, Blade Master. In the long run you'll be part of that. There will be a lot of dying happening at that meeting, that's for sure. What concerns us is there are some not scheduled to pass on just yet."

"What do you mean?" Talaza asked, his curiosity increasing.

"We are looking for two individuals and some information," Uniss said. "One of those we seek looks bit like I do: same height, a little thinner, except he's dressed all in brown. Has a hat and heavy coat bit like this too." Uniss pointed to his own broad-brimmed dark-blue hat and gray duster. "Only his is brown. He goes by the name Starlin. He's dangerous—very dangerous."

Talaza studied the dark hat jammed down low over Uniss's brow, with its wide crown and a silver band—a style like none Talaza had ever seen in Ludd.

Waiting for Talaza to speak next, Uniss just stood there, with one hand in the pocket of his gray broad-collared shin-length coat. With the coat open at the front, Talaza could see the rough blue-dyed trousers that covered the Star Lord's legs. They were held up by a wide belt and buckle that bore a clan coat of arms whose heraldry was unknown to Talaza. Scuffed black military-style boots bore witness to many hard miles.

Maybe he was the one controlling the glowing beetle-shaped object Analuke and I saw settle to ground before?

"Have you seen anyone like that in your travels recently?" Dogg asked, breaking the silence.

Talaza shook his head.

"The second individual we are looking for is . . ." Uniss paused. ". . . you."

Talaza felt a shiver of concern wash over him.

"I'm sorry, my friend," said Uniss. "We can't let you take part in what is about to unfold back there. Can't afford to have you pass on. You'll have to sit this one out. You're too important to the future."

Talaza's eyes widened as his mind jumped to Analuke. He swallowed down the worry he felt rising within. "What of Analuke?" he asked. "You cannot ask me to abandon her."

Uniss shook his head. "Her path takes a different direction, and the outcome is uncertain. We'll do what we can to see she gets where she needs to go safely. But if you interfere, you will guarantee her end as sure as you are standing here."

Uniss's voice had authority to it, but it felt like the voice of someone who could be trusted—someone who knew his way around this life, perhaps even something beyond. Talaza regarded this Uniss carefully. He stood equal in stature to most Flaxon males—Talaza had eliminated many of *them* in the past.

Talaza straightened his posture, thinking, considering Uniss's dark skin and eyes. *Not fair and green-eyed like a Flaxon of Weirawind, and his coverings . . . far too different. My bones say he is telling the truth. Oh my, he is the Star Lord.*

"As I said, my name's Uniss, and this is my obviously intelligent offsider, Dogg." He expressed these words with a broad grin as he crouched next to Dogg.

Then, pressing his palms together, Uniss placed the tips of his fingers against his lips thoughtfully.

"I think we can help each other, Blade Master," he said. "Could I know your true name?"

"The true name of a Quall is never spoken to a Kurja, Star Lord or not," Talaza said.

Uniss tossed Dogg a wry smile, then rose and shifted his view back to the Quall. "I reckon your clan calls you . . . let me see, Talaza—Blade Master of Black Mountain. Would that be right?"

Talaza stepped back in surprise—not only because Uniss already knew Talaza's name, but even more because Uniss's words had been spoken flawlessly in Talaza's own Black Mountain dialect.

"That is a tongue no Kurja had ever been permitted to learn!" Talaza said. "How is it you speak our words? They are closed to Kurja!"

Dogg wagged her tail, to draw Talaza's attention. "We know many things about your clan and your world, Talaza."

Uniss closed the gap between himself and Talaza, extending a hand. Talaza gazed at the hand and then Uniss's eyes. Finally Talaza accepted the gesture as amicable, offering his own upper right hand.

Uniss nodded. "There is much death soon to occur on this world, and you cannot be part of that. You have a greater part to play, my brave friend."

"You must allow me to help Analuke," Talaza said. "Please."

Uniss regarded Talaza with compassion. "I've told you what I have for good reason, Blade Master. Her final place at the end of this day's events is still unclear, even to us. Analuke has decisions to make—decisions you can't be part of."

"She will make a good account of herself and uphold the honor of your clan," Dogg said.

This is why my bones are aching. He took a slow breath. "I may never see her again. Is this your meaning, Star Lord?"

"She lives in your heart," Uniss said. "Carry that for now."

Talaza felt a great in-rush of air followed by an explosive upward surge of energy mixed with the sound of shattering crystal. Shafts of silver light rose from the ground, enveloping all three of them. Talaza's stomach lurched as he felt his body somehow become vaporous, merging with the light stream. Then, as if he became the wind itself, Talaza and the other two began to ascend skyward, and vanished.

*****

Moments later, from around the bend came the glow of torchlight. With it came the sound of many riders—clinking harnesses and plodding hooves. Out of the gloom emerged a column of twenty Flaxon. Each soldier wore a polished metal cuirass and heavy linen trousers of crimson. The company passed through the space completely unaware of the meeting that had occurred only moments before. The leading officer raised a hand and drew the column to a halt.

In the distance they heard the shrill whistle of a tiny bird. The sound ended with a tap, as though someone had struck a broadhead nail with a hammer. Without a word he dropped his hand and the column plodded on.

CHAPTER

4

Knife Edge

In the forest at the mouth of the pass, Analuke scouted the area in overlapping circles beneath the moons' light. Soon after Talaza had departed, she noticed that the night birds stopped calling. Then she also became aware that all the foraging animals native to the forest were silent too.

Oh dear.

Somewhere in the distance the whispered murmur of an unintelligible voice on the breeze caught her ear. Believing their targets to be near, she sent a bird-whistle arrow into the air toward the pass mouth, as Talaza had instructed.

Why does this place feel so on edge?

Close around her Analuke felt a sudden unworldly drop in temperature. From her left, a sheet of mist passed over her, carrying the putrid smell of decaying flesh. Again she heard murmured words that chilled her to the bone.

Where are you, husband?

She decided to begin her return, feeling her will to maintain her chameleon effect declining. Some yards on, intuition told her to stop. She crouched quietly beside a hut-sized boulder matted with rust-colored lichen and moss. A faint sound of steps from the other side of the boulder caught her ear.

Cautiously, Analuke leaned to peer around the corner. She froze, feeling a large living force very close to her.

In the next moment, with a brief sound of static and a shimmer of light, a muscular leg clad in familiar black slaa-woven trousers materialized. Right next to her face, the heavy boot of a ten-foot-tall Scarzen Maximum Sentinel pressed down upon the ground in near silence. The warrior's attention was squarely fixed on the entrance to Yorr Pass. Analuke had seen the Scarzen blur skill used many times, but she had never been caught as unprepared as this. His leg measured almost as long as she was tall.

Ever so carefully, Analuke withdrew. She knew she was looking at one of the most feared of the Scarzen warriors, a true destroyer of the enemy on any battlefield. She pressed all apprehension to the back of her mind, steeling herself to be ready to fight for her life. The sentinel's boot knife, a mere backup, was sheathed in a calf scabbard. Its blade stretched almost as long as one of her arms.

Analuke swallowed, readying herself to move. Slowly, her two bottom hands reached for a pair of scuttling blades from the cluster of others low on her belt. She could feel the will feeding her chameleon camouflage being consumed at a horrendous rate. Analuke raised her view to see the fearsome angular features of the typically unprotected Scarzen's face. She noted he had dreadlock war braids bearing symbols of Talon East Bunker. She knew by the braids that this one was not an officer. That meant more of their unit or company were not far away—two more, if Elder Makayass's information proved correct. The sentinel's torso was clad in elite drommal-hide armor, with black slaa-cloth sleeves and war gauntlets. In his right fist the warrior carried a gem-encrusted mace, its crushing ball larger than Analuke's head. The haft of the weapon was embossed with the strange Chicaa script of the Scarzen, likely in recognition of a former ancestor.

In the wind from behind her, she heard a low, menacing laugh, then: "They're coming," she heard a voice say.

The speaker's tone had a deranged, almost joyful anticipation.

The unfamiliar voice so close took Analuke by surprise and made her feel surrounded. Her hands gripped the handle of her blades unnaturally tight. Behind and to her left, Analuke heard a tiny whistle. She shifted her view to see who'd made the sound. Her heart jumped at seeing another Scarzen only several strides away, looking directly across to her position. This one had the orange eyes that legend said could burn a hole right through a body.

That's two, so one more yet hidden—where are they? she mused.

Analuke saw a broad blade sheathed on the second Scarzen's hip, with a magnificent gold-braided grip and jewel-studded pommel. His long dreadlocks at the back of his head were bound into a ponytail, with red ribbon woven through. Analuke felt a rush. She recognized the gold bands adorning his separate ear-braids—multiples. An officer—and one of significant rank.

The target? she wondered. *Has to be.*

Shorter than the one next to her by a head or two, the officer was imposing nonetheless in his immaculate black-and-tan slaa weave gambeson.

Again she heard a whisper on the wind: "Danger."

That baleful voice chilled her more than being discovered by the bone-breaker standing right beside her. She held her position still as stone, convincing herself that the voice could be a Scarzen mind game—something they used to flush wily spies from cover. Elite Scarzen warriors possessed battlefield skills that extended far beyond their bodies being precision weapons.

She focused on the officer, her critical target, planning the next steps in his elimination. She could make out the military insignia of Talon East embossed into the upper right of his body armor—a gold-leaf tree over crossed war axes.

A fine trophy, she thought, *and evidence of the kill.*

A noise drew the Scarzen officer's attention. He swung his view away from Analuke's position toward the pass. It sounded like the call of a night ploot, but too regular for it to be the small avian.

The Scarzen officer responded with a different soft whistle and then a hand signal to the warrior near Analuke. Away to the left she now saw another Scarzen uncloak, placing her amidst the three of them. The third one had a narrow face and was slighter in build than the more heavily armored individual close to her. He was likewise devoid of command rank and carried a pole-arm bearing a cruel flame-shaped blade on each end.

Mmm, likes to be in the fray. That weapon measures about five of my long steps. Must use it for close-quarter combat.

Just then, opposite Analuke's position, the snorting of a horse in the near distance caused all eyes to shift in the direction of the pass. The Scarzen officer signaled his larger subordinate to move to a wider flank. He responded immediately, applying his blur skill, then Analuke watched as his form faded to a shimmer. She breathed a sigh of relief when she heard his first few soft steps fade into the distance. Only because she had a direct bead on the warrior's residual was Analuke able to watch the sentinel move off. Silently he approached a large stendle tree some twenty paces away, where his camouflage blended fully into the rough bark. A quick look to the other two saw them make no attempt to conceal themselves.

Perhaps they have ambush in mind? she wondered. *That makes it harder. Alright then, eliminate the big one first, keep him off my back, then the officer.*

The sound of hooves met Analuke's ears. Back toward the pass she saw the silhouette of three mounted riders break through a pocket of underbrush and rolling mist.

Flaxon.

The Scarzen officer and the other visible warrior who had clearly seen them too, stepped forward and made themselves obvious. Then, faintly in the background, Analuke saw vague shadows moving to left and right flanks.

Flaxon foot soldiers. She grimaced. *Why do open faces always think the darkness conceals their true intentions? Have they not learned how well a Scarzen sees at night? So much for three a side,* she thought while carefully unsheathing two more blades. *They are about to start.* She looked to the pass. *Husband, where are you?*

Seeing no sign of him, Analuke wondered for a moment if he'd been discovered and dealt with. Her mood darkened, and she moved toward her first target as the two enemy groups converged.

Act 2

CHAPTER

5

No Turning Back

Major Bollard was a seasoned commander of the Ninth Regiment Flaxon Light Horse. He was also first cousin to Flaxor's regent, Trabonus. He had fought against the Scarzen twice in recent times at the Battle of South Dam on their southern border. A while later he found himself in a position to volunteer himself and his assigned company for this mission. Consistent with Flaxon church rhetoric and ideology, Bollard saw all Scarzen as an enemy that needed to be put down in any way possible. Flaxor's southern nemesis was held as a barbaric sub-life form under demonic influence. The doctrine of the Flaxon one god of creation and universal balance taught: *"Scarzen are a scourge never to be trusted. They must be pacified by whatever means available down to the last Flaxon. It is the duty of every Flaxon to ensure peace and prosperity for the races of Ludd and the greater world of Tora."*

In keeping with this directive, the orders handed down to Bollard were explicit:

Step One: Lure the Scarzen in. Offer them the design for the secret Screwshot water pump in exchange for cessation of guerilla raids on the new Flaxon dam project. Make overtures for expanding Flaxon borders into the north passage.

Step Two: While the parley is taking place, surround the Scarzen. Kill them. Search the dead. Recover any of the blue healing liquid they are known to carry.

Step Three: Leave evidence of Chou treachery on one of the dead.

Step Four: Return immediately to Weirawind. Deliver the prize directly to me.

The orders were signed and wax-sealed by Regent Trabonus himself.

***

Unknown to Major Bollard, the Scarzen commander facing them was one O'Rexuss Titarliaa, chief of security for Talon East Bunker, and Titarliaa had plans of his own to follow. Almost without falter, the Scarzen lived by their word. They had arrived as agreed, numbering only three. The guidelines of Titarliaa's mission came at the behest of High Keeper Malforce, navigator and supreme leader of Talon East.

Titarliaa's own hatred for the Flaxon stemmed from their consistent lack of honor on the battlefield—that, as well as their callous oppression of Scarza's western ally, the Celeron. His orders were also simple:

Take the Flaxon commanding officer hostage. Consult with and eliminate the rest. Later, interrogate the commander as to key strong and weak positions in and around Weirawind City. Find out all you can about this black powder of thunder our spies have reported. Relieve the officer of his ability to breathe.

A veteran of many warring campaigns against the Flaxon and other enemies of Scarza, Commander Titarliaa had come expecting to be double-crossed. Once that occurred, he intended to consult with the Flaxon in the extreme.

I'll put a head or two in a bag and hang them on one of Weirawind City's walls as a clear sign of disapproval.

Commander Titarliaa stood there, impassive, watching them draw closer.

They have threatened the existence of our irreplaceable orchids, and by extension, our Scarzen heart. I hope they get to their treachery with haste. I'd like to get to the killing as soon as possible.

The mounted Flaxon rode forward, exuding confidence.

Titarliaa's jaw tightened. *Only when they have strength in numbers will they act so bold.* "Let them come," he said under his breath.

About to advance toward them to force a beginning to the meeting, Titarliaa paused, noticing a tiny wild orchid growing from under a flat rock.

Oh, your natural climb for sunlight is restricted. Let me help you.

Ignoring the approaching horsemen, Titarliaa knelt down and pulled the oppressive stone aside to give the orchid a chance as his aide stopped next to him.

"Bring spirit to this land," Titarliaa whispered, brushing the flower's petals with care. Looking up to the riders again, he stood. "Now to business," he said in their direction.

As Commander Titarliaa and his aide, Norexx, strode forward, they saw no sign of supporting Flaxon troops, but experience told Titarliaa they would be there. Suspicious, Titarliaa scanned the flanks of the approaching riders.

"There is a consult in this, Norexx—I can feel it," Titarliaa told his aide via the mind tether that all Scarzen shared in close range. *"Ready your kin. Hurl no barrier or blade until my order. When that happens, all breathe their last except their commander. He is to be interrogated."*

"As you command," Norexx replied, his words echoing his usual unwavering commitment to his commander.

Then they waited for the Flaxon to make the next move.

CHAPTER

6

Killing Ground

Stark moonlight lit the ground where the forest canopy was absent around Analuke. A short distance east of Titarliaa's position, she closed in behind her first target. She knew that, to Scarzen eyes, her chameleon skill offered small protection while she was in motion. Staying low, taking great care to use every bit of natural cover, Analuke closed the gap. She knew she would have only one chance at the sentinel. His advantages would dominate the exchange if she got a fraction of her surprise attack wrong.

Talaza must be in position to take out the Flaxon target by now, she thought.

Analuke still saw her target's blur skill residual against the broad stendle trunk. The dark shadows around him, however, made it difficult to discern which way he was facing. Blades ready, she hoped she was looking at the Scarzen face on. Just then, her focus was drawn to her left as a curt exchange began between the two converging parties.

"You are the representative," said the Scarzen commander—his words more statement than question.

The Flaxon officer straightened in the saddle. Analuke watched the Scarzen commander and his aide halt the Flaxon advance. The two parties eyed each other for a small moment.

"I am Major Bollard, if you must know. I represent Regent Trabonus of Flaxor. Who is the servant I address?"

Analuke watched the Scarzen officer study the Flaxon in silence.

Probably sizing him up for the kill, she mused. She crept forward. Just for a moment, in the short distance on the other side of the clearing, she thought she glimpsed another figure.

Tall like a Flaxon, she thought, *but not clad like a Flaxon wearing such an odd hat and long coat.*

Analuke's eyes darted away from the mysterious figure when she noticed the Scarzen sentinel moving silently to the near side of the tree trunk. His maneuver caused her to change her own direction, forcing her uncomfortably close to the unfolding parley. When she looked for the long-coated figure again, he was gone.

Then a soft rustle in the undergrowth caught her attention on the far side of her target. Since Analuke heard it, she knew the Scarzen did too.

Definitely not Talaza, she thought. *He'd never be so clumsy.* Her stomach churned. *Oh my, this doesn't feel right at all.*

The Scarzen officer finally responded to Major Bollard: "Scarzen have no servants—only warriors. My name is Titarliaa, a Scarzen of rank respectable enough to represent Malforce, High Keeper of Talon East. This is my aide Norexx."

So . . . Titarliaa? You are my primary target, then, Analuke thought.

"Are you three in number as agreed?" Titarliaa said.

"Starting the parley with mistrust is a poor sign of goodwill, my dear Titarliaa," Bollard said. "But then I suppose good manners will be as rare as good character amongst your . . . whatever you are."

"Two-faced dishonorable drommal turds," Norexx muttered in his native tongue.

"What did he say?" Bollard said.

"He said . . ." Titarliaa paid Norexx a glance. "He said your mounts make you look so much taller."

Analuke watched Titarliaa crouch down, clearly feeling no threat from their mutual long-time enemy. He picked a wildflower and twiddled it in his hand.

"And you," Bollard said. "Where is your third?"

Still crouching, Titarliaa looked at the flower in his hand. "Close by, I assure you," he said. "They are keeping an eye out for hostile wildlife. Dangerous in this part of the forest, you know." Titarliaa looked up at Bollard. "Never know what might jump out of the underbrush to bite you."

Analuke looked on as one of the Flaxon officers to Bollard's right shifted uncomfortably in his saddle.

"What exactly are you implying?" Bollard asked.

Now the Scarzen commander looked hard at the Flaxon. "You speak of mistrust? Scarzen are known across Ludd for being a race who keep their word. Flaxon are reported to have more . . . color in their behavior. Are we here to parley, or are you just here to fart in your saddle?"

Bollard grunted and mumbled something under his breath.

"The stingers will be out when the deep evening comes," Titarliaa said. "I'd prefer to keep them at bay and talk by a warm fire. Will you dismount to speak on equal terms, representative of Flaxor?"

"Do you take me for a fool, Scarzen? I will address you eye to eye."

"If that's easier on your nerves, Major Broznard," Titarliaa said, "by all means remain on top of your animal."

"Can I eviscerate them now, sir?" muttered Norexx in the Scarzen tongue.

Analuke had to smile this time—both at Norexx's ongoing vexation and Titarliaa's clearly purposeful butchering of Bollard's name.

"Now what is your aide jabbering about, Titarliaa?" Bollard asked.

"He said that you each look like you've been in the saddle too long and your legs need stretching."

Amused by the dark exchange, Analuke watched Titarliaa stand slowly and place his feet apart in a balanced stance. In this position he truly was looking at the Flaxon commander eye to eye.

Analuke suddenly sensed that something had shifted in the parley.

"Let's waste no more time, Major Broznard," Titarliaa said. "What terms have you to table?"

Bollard shuffled in his saddle and glanced to the nearest officer on his right.

"His name is Major Bollard, Scarzen," said the officer. "You will do well to remember that."

Bollard sighed and lifted a placating hand. "Thank you, Masters. We are here for a diplomatic outcome, remember." He looked back at the Scarzen. "Commander Titarliaa, the regent of Flaxor is aware that Scarza's water supply is dwindling. The water levels of our own fair Flaxor's lands are dropping also. Hence the recent need to dam our reserves. Our regent also realizes that somehow this may have impacted your own lands. In his compassion Regent Trabonus seeks to extend a helping hand, though I personally fail to see why— but then here we are."

Titarliaa raised one eyebrow. "The water supply, really? Is that it?"

"Why . . . yes," Bollard replied. "Isn't that enough? Was there some other matter that held your concern? That is what you have been fighting for, killing our innocents for this past year and more, isn't it?"

Titarliaa leaned forward just a bit. "Let me give you a little advice, Major, something I rarely do for one such as yourself. Play your word traps with a lighter touch; it will enhance your credibility. What do you really want?"

The other horsemen shifted their posture, clearly uncomfortable at the Scarzen's attitude, all while Analuke continued to move to her target.

"Very well," Bollard said. "Truth is, we hope to put our differences aside. Regent Trabonus's larger view is that we must not destroy ourselves through war or starvation. He believes we can both avoid much suffering by sharing the deep-water resources of the underground rivers that traverse our lands and the Neutral Zone."

"Go on," Titarliaa said.

"Yeah, keep digging, broz," mumbled Norexx.

From her position to the right of the exchange, Analuke continued to listen and watch. She could feel an ongoing subtle escalation in the tension between the two parties and knew it was only a matter of time.

This is not going well, she thought.

Bollard then extended a hand to the subordinate on his right without turning that way. "Give!" Bollard ordered.

The soldier passed Bollard a leather cylinder. By that moment, Analuke had managed to creep within striking distance of her first target. She stopped. She then began to wonder how she would cross the open patch of ground for the final strike on Titarliaa, her primary mark. The moment she struck down the sentinel, Analuke knew the Scarzen commander would take unpredictable measures of his own.

She watched as Bollard pulled a rolled parchment from the cylinder, then unfurl it and read from the scroll, "Consistent with the letter of hope we have compassionately responded to, Regent Trabonus offers plans for a new deep-lift siphon that will enable our Scarzen . . . *neighbors* to irrigate their fields with endless water."

"Neighbors?" Norexx muttered. "We've more in common with the wild drommal herds than them. What was he ingesting before he arrived?"

Titarliaa shot Norexx a glance, then said to Bollard, "Umm, letter of hope *we* responded to?" Titarliaa enquired.

Bollard looked up from the scroll, an annoyed look on his face. "That's what I said, didn't I? Weren't you listening? You're making this all very difficult, Titarliaa. I shouldn't be surprised." Bollard looked at his two accompanying officers. "No appreciation for the value of something precious, even when it's put right in front of them." Bollard rolled up the parchment hastily and shoved it back into the cylinder. "The plans are in there as well."

Bollard extended his arm to hand the cylinder to the Scarzen commander, but Titarliaa held his position, making no move to accept it.

"Give you a moment to think about it, shall I?" Bollard said.

"You know, Major, I find you a most disagreeable envoy," Titarliaa said.

Bollard tossed the cylinder at Titarliaa's feet. "Do we have an agreement or not?"

Analuke cringed. *Oh, that wasn't wise. Never force a Scarzen's hand.*

She noticed a sheet of mist disperse through the trees forward left of her position. For a moment she thought she glimpsed movement in the underbrush. Just then Commander Titarliaa, ignoring the cylinder on the ground and stepped close enough to touch Commander Bollard's mount on the head. Then Norexx moved forward and recovered the cylinder.

"And in return for this . . . gesture?" Titarliaa asked, touching the horse gently on the muzzle.

"Peace, of course," Bollard said. "Our neighbors to the west, the Celeron, have told us many times that Scarzen live by their word of promise. This you also have so kindly reminded us earlier. Regent Trabonus asks only for your pledge and mark on parchment. He asks you agree that the border of the Neutral Zone will be expanded in Flaxor's favor by a march of two thousand standard steps, south toward the Lyran Mountains."

Norexx scoffed, then coughed and with a hand over his mouth muffled an obscenity at the Flaxon.

As if the terms were already acceptable, Bollard extended a hand to the officer on his right, who passed Bollard a second cylinder. The major in turn offered it to Titarliaa.

Standing eye to eye with the mounted major, Titarliaa accepted the proffered cylinder, easily reaching for it over the horse's head.

With everyone's attention on the Scarzen officer, Analuke knew this was her one chance to strike. She moved in toward the concealed Scarzen sentinel standing against the tree until she was only steps away. About to take her final action, she heard the faint crack of a stick to her right. Her attention shifted toward the noise. *What was that?*

Seeing nothing, Analuke looked back to the sentinel, and felt a distinct change their demeanor. Then, in the underbrush beyond them, she saw movement, a figure on two legs—a soldier. She saw the head of a crossbow lifted to the aim position, pointing across the way—toward the Scarzen commander.

If they loose and miss, everyone dies she thought.

With a smooth backhand she released a blade, aiming high, and it struck its target with a *thunk*. Next came a gagging sound and the crossbow dropped. A

Flaxon fell forward through the bushes, holding his throat, landing face-first in the dirt.

The noise shattered the focus of everyone in the parley. Titarliaa half turned toward the fallen soldier, a hand on his long knife.

"Assassin!" shouted one of the mounted Flaxon. "Betrayal! We are attacked!"

With everyone's attention on the fallen Flaxon soldier, Analuke snapped her view right to see her large Scarzen target uncloak. In that moment her shift in focus and weakening will saw her own camouflage dissolve. The full weight of the Scarzen sentinel's attention fell on her. Cold and calculating, he stepped forward and raised his war mace overhead, preparing to end her. But instead of shrinking away from her attacker, Analuke reached for another blade.

"Come for me, Scarzen," she growled, launching herself at the giant.

As the sentinel drove his mace downward in a vicious crushing blow, Analuke skillfully somersaulted out of the way of the deadly swing. Landing, without hesitation she threw her first blade, which bit deep into the sentinel's outer thigh. She ran at the Scarzen, stepping on the knife for leverage. The shock and unexpected pain from the embedded blade caused the Scarzen sentinel to arch back with a cry of pain. Analuke used the blades in her other three hands to stab-climb up the sentinel's torso while her empty hand reached for a new weapon.

In a heartbeat Analuke sprung to the top of his chest, landing on her right foot. Using her left foot, she drove his shoulder back with a jarring kick before she side-flipped away. In midair she hurled two blades that found their mark— one in each of his eye sockets. Analuke landed with perfect balance as the heavy body of her victim fell face-first and lifeless to the ground with a crash.

"Sir! Enemy to our left!" yelled one of Bollard's subordinates pointing.

"Once again you Flaxon show your lack of spine," Titarliaa spat.

The prime target now facing her, Analuke set off toward him drawing another two blades. A war cry from her right caused her steps to falter as instinct forced her head low. She barely avoided a Flaxon trident thrown by a soldier, one of many emerging from the underbrush shadows. She went to step-off again and the ground collapsed under the weight of her foot. A Barfanark's burrow swallowed her leg to the mid-shin and the fall twisted her ankle, momentarily halting her charge. Scrambling to her feet, she saw Major Bollard reach into his jacket. He brought into view a shiny instrument of metal and wood, which he pointed deliberately at the back of Titarliaa's head. Despite the fact that Titarliaa could see Bollard's actions through Norexx's eyes via their mind-tether, there was no time to react.

Analuke saw a flash, followed by a *crack-bang*, and Titarliaa bellowed in pain as the rest of the Flaxon closed in from two sides. Titarliaa lurched forward, a hand clasping the back of his head and fell to one knee. Clearly Bollard's attack had maimed the Scarzen, but not killed him. Realizing Titarliaa still lived, callously, Bollard dug his spurs in rearing his horse intending to trample Titarliaa and finish the job. As the animal's iron-shod hooves fell, they struck Titarliaa's unprotected back, driving him hard to the ground.

Now in considerable pain, Analuke stayed low, watching as Bollard wheeled his horse around for another strike. But before Bollard could complete his maneuver, Norexx leapt to his commander's defense using a repel barrier to shove Titarliaa to one side. In that moment, another of the mounted Flaxon drew a flash-bang weapon of his own and pointed it at Norexx.

At the same time, Norexx drew upon his will forming a repel barrier in one hand and hurled the ballistic force at the Flaxon. The full force of the barrier narrowly missed the soldier, but the brush of its force still managed to knock him off his horse and send him scrambling in retreat.

Analuke watched Norexx hurl another repel field, this time at Bollard, who was already charging back toward Titarliaa. Norexx's field struck Bollard in the chest, unhorsing him and sending him sprawling to the ground.

By that time, Titarliaa had managed to regain his feet looking for revenge. Analuke watched as the last mounted Flaxon aimed his own weapon at the head of Titarliaa, shouting "You die, beast!"

With a skillful maneuver of breathtaking speed and agility, Titarliaa ducked while drawing a dagger from his hip belt with his left hand. Using an aggressive forehand motion, Titarliaa flung the blade at the chest of the Flaxon's mount. The blade sank deep between the horse's ribs. Screaming in pain, the horse reared and fell sideways, throwing its rider. As the Flaxon hit the ground, the weapon in his hand discharged.

Analuke saw the now familiar flash and heard the *crack-bang* from the weapon as many more Flaxon spilled into the clearing from the shadows. The world suddenly slowed for Analuke as she felt the impact of a molten hot force strike her chest. She reeled, bleeding hard as she watched a melee of kin barriers, flying arrows, and clashing blades. Bollard's company now threw themselves at her and the two surviving Scarzen committed to the last man.

Analuke heard shouts and troops charging in her direction through the undergrowth. A repel field sizzled past her, slamming into a nearby tree spraying splintered bark over her.

Determined and grim-faced, the Flaxon soldiers closed on her, armed to the teeth with short tridents, long knives, and bucklers. She counted nine, three charging directly at her, and three on each of her flanks.

"Kill it quick, lads!" ordered a Flaxon sergeant leading the charge.

Bellowing a chilling Quall war cry, Analuke spun, hurling three knives striking the throats of the three in front. She rolled right and snatched three more blades from their scabbards. Then she stepped aside just in time to dodge the thrust of a trident from one direction and a thrown axe from another. She leapt and fed a blade into the mouth of the next aggressor who'd stepped in to cut her down. Flipping sideways, landing unsteadily on her injured ankle, Analuke whipped her head around, slapping another closing enemy across the eyes with her poisoned ponytail. The soldier screamed and fell to the ground with hands covering his bleeding face.

Feeling herself fading she looked for escape. She ducked the swing of a trident, then dropped, spun, and ground-swept her attacker. With a vicious forward swing, she sliced open the leg of another, hitting his femoral artery. Standing to deal with her next adversary, she was struck in the back by a large boot. The force drove her face first into the dirt. Winded and in severe pain, Analuke lifted her head slowly to see Commander Titarliaa step over her. One side of his face was covered in blood, but he was smiling, like he was about to join a celebration. Analuke knew that when a Scarzen smiled, a lot of dying on the part of the enemy was about to take place.

"Come, vermin!" the Scarzen commander bellowed at the remaining Flaxon. "See what Titarliaa has for you!"

Bursting through the underbrush from the opposite flank, a second wave of soldiers charged into the fray.

Titarliaa laughed. "Yes! Let's consult with gusto, shall we?"

With all the Flaxon now focused on Titarliaa, Analuke used the distraction to attempt to crawl to cover. Exhausted, she stopped near the dead sentinel she had eliminated earlier and rolled on her back. From that position, she watched the Scarzen commander advance on the first of four Flaxon who'd surrounded him—not far from where Norexx engaged a host of Flaxon on his own. A crushing side-kick from Titarliaa struck the soldier so hard in the chest that it killed him outright. The force launched the lifeless form through the air to strike a tree with a sickening thud.

"That's one!" Titarliaa shouted. "Come on! A little more effort, please."

Two Flaxon charged him at once, brandishing their tridents. Using the spine of his long knife, Titarliaa parried the first offensive thrust. Bringing his blade around, he then removed the head of one soldier with a diagonal downward cut. With a shout the second soldier struck low, aiming for Titarliaa's pelvis—a heart shot to a Scarzen, Analuke knew. But instead of a deathblow, the sharp tines of his trident failed to make any penetration to the solid wall of bone under the armor. In reply Titarliaa brought his blade down across the shaft of the trident, severing it clean with the single ringing sound of a bell. The Flaxon cried out in fear before Titarliaa split him down the center, leaving the two halves to fall untidily to ground.

Then Analuke saw Titarliaa apply his blur skill, and a wave of trepidation washed over her for the carnage she knew would follow. The prowess, speed, and ferocity with which the Scarzen dissected each advancing enemy was awe-inspiring, even for a seasoned Quall assassin like Analuke.

Titarliaa turned his attention toward Norexx, who was surrounded and was consulting with more than his fair share of opponents.

"Come on, Norexx!" Titarliaa shouted. "Stop toying with them. We have work to do."

"Applying myself now, sir," said Norexx, decapitating two luckless Flaxon with a single stroke.

In a matter of seconds, Norexx dealt with his last assailants and then silence filled the space. Here and there, blood spatter and parts of Flaxon dead littered the forest floor.

Analuke looked toward the remaining two Scarzen, who appeared unharmed and composed, despite the violence of moments before. She wanted to flee, but with her injuries as severe as the were, that was impossible.

"Sir, your head," Norexx said. "You have suffered an injury."

Titarliaa reached to the back of his head with one hand and winced.

"May I suggest we treat it now, sir?"

Titarliaa considered the smear of blood on his glove, the unusual expression on his face could have easily been interpreted as one of puzzlement. He dismissed the injury with a wave of his bloodied hand. "I told you there was a consult in this. I've not had the pleasure of killing an honorable one of them yet."

Analuke watched Commander Titarliaa survey his surroundings. His gaze swept across the battleground, halting abruptly when he saw her lying near one of his own fallen.

Oh . . . kark, she thought feeling sure these would be the last moments of her life.

Titarliaa strode to where she lay. With Norexx standing behind him, Titarliaa knelt down next to Analuke and looked at her for a moment. Taking a silver flask from his utility belt, he removed the lid and lifted a small clump of wadding from inside the cap. With care he applied the blue-stained wet material to a nasty cut on Analuke's arm. The wound and the surrounding area radiated blue for a short moment before she saw the cut close and heal completely.

"I think I see now what the game was," Titarliaa said to her. "How many are you? Who sent you?"

Analuke said nothing, but just stared squarely into the strength of Titarliaa's orange eyes.

"You know," he said, "I want to share with you a small secret. I actually respect you Quall. In fact Scarzen in general do. You stick to your contract. You strike only those who are guilty in the eyes of your employer while ensuring they are capable of defending themselves. You are also known to reverse the contract on the employer if they are discovered to have played you false. I admire that."

Analuke swallowed hard to speak through her dry mouth. "All beings have their purpose."

"So true," replied Titarliaa and then looked to his fallen subordinate. "You killed my friend over there—a tough job. He was one of my best and has never been defeated by any outside our clan. So tell me, who sent you to this mutual trap? And on my word as a Scarzen, your unethical employer will pay for their dishonorable conduct."

Analuke, though, only wondered about Talaza. *What has happened to him?*

She attempted to speak, but her voice lacked the strength.

Titarliaa leaned in closer.

"Heal me," she croaked, looking down to her chest where the Flaxon weapon had injured her. She was clearly bleeding badly. "And I will tell you."

Titarliaa shook his head. "I'm sorry, my little friend. I only offered a small amount, as too much trilix will only damn your spirit to never reach your hall of ancestors. Tell me who your deceiver is and I will avenge your name."

"Wang So Tan," Analuke whispered. "It was Wang So Tan."

Titarliaa raised an eyebrow in obvious surprise, looked up at Norexx, and then nodded. "Makes sense."

He looked back at Analuke. "You speak true and I will honor my part. Norexx, see that her body gets back to the foot of Black Mountain, where she will be found by her kind. Place her in a respectful way and say a prayer for her spirit to be guided to her hall of ancestors."

"It will be done as ordered. And you, sir?" Norexx asked, scooping Analuke up in both arms.

She almost passed out as he picked her up.

"I will return to Talon East," Titarliaa said. "Keeper Malforce will want to hear the news of what has happened here and decide what has to be done."

"As you wish," said Norexx, turning away.

As Norexx walked off with Analuke in his arms, she looked back toward Titarliaa, seeing him treat his own wound with the trilix-soaked wadding.

In her fading consciousness and anguish, Analuke's last thoughts were of her Talaza. Her heart reached out for him. Then, like a fading light, she left this world for a new beginning.

CHAPTER

7

Interlocking Circles

Talaza awoke in a mental haze. The smell of a campfire and the low murmur of voices stirred him to full consciousness.

It was still dark as his eyes opened. He rolled his head to one side, feeling some sort of padding under his body, and then touched the material supporting him. He had been placed on a bed of bracken. Opposite he saw the Star Lord, Uniss, sitting on a log. The strange talking canine Uniss referred to as "Dogg" sat beside the small fire nearby. Then Talaza became aware that both were entirely focused on him.

"Ah, good, you're awake," Uniss said. "Sit yourself up. We have to talk."

Talaza pushed himself to a sitting position and looked around. He noticed that his knife belts had been neatly positioned on the ground beside him, everything intact.

"Where are we?" Talaza asked. Then his eyes widened and he snapped a look around. "Analuke! Where is Analuke?"

Uniss sighed removing his hat. He placed it next to him on the log with care and then looked at Dogg.

"I hate this part, Dogg." Uniss lifted his view to Talaza. "There was quite a scrap after we left, I'm sorry to say. We had hoped that sanity might have prevailed. We were wrong."

Uniss threaded his fingers together with an expression of someone about to hand down grim news.

"What do you mean?" Talaza asked eyes narrowing.

"From what we saw," Uniss said, "in the skirmish there was a nasty turn of events between the Flaxon and the Scarzen. Some we knew would die today, but there were others whose life should have been spared . . . including your Analuke."

Talaza's eyes softened. "You mean she's . . ."

"She did make a good account of herself, as I promised," Dogg said gently.

"You were there?" Talaza asked, his voice cracking.

"Yes," Dogg said. "To the end."

Talaza eyes filled with tears and he felt his stomach lurch. "Why did you not leave me there? Her path was my path!"

Uniss frowned and then shook his head. "Nah. It was—"

"You still have two sons who must play their part in things to come," Dogg interrupted. "They need you more than ever now."

Uniss nodded. "There's events to come involving certain individuals. Were you not here to influence some of their decision making, their life's course will not unfold as it should."

"Bah!" Talaza snapped. "How do you know the future? You are not Hex! How can you know such things?"

"It is our job to know, Blade Master," Uniss said.

Talaza wiped at his tears with the back of one hand, clenching the others into fists. "How can I give worth to Analuke's passing now? If death was our path, we should have departed together!"

Uniss glanced at Dogg. "You're right Talaza: we are not Hex. But we do know some of what is to come. Before you return to your mountain, there are actions you can take that *may* ease some of your pain."

Talaza stood and glared at Uniss. "What actions?" he asked. "Quall law now applies. By her name all guilty in the crime are now legitimate targets of all Quall. I claim my right of vengeance. Let Hex judge me when it's my time."

Uniss raised a hand. "Now hang on a minute, Blade Master. There are several things we need to consider. We don't want more innocents suffering."

"There are no innocents in this!" Talaza said stabbing a finger towards Uniss.

***

Uniss looked at Dogg, opening a telepathic bridge. *"He's right, you know, Dogg."*

"Uniss, we can't let this go further. We must guide his intent for vengeance into a workable alternative. I suggest we use Plan B."

Uniss glanced at Talaza, who shook with mounting rage, clearly waiting for some response.

"We still have to bring our new apprentice from Earth into these events and see where Ben's part fits in all this too," Dogg continued. *"We know he is also linked to Talaza. We can't afford to have the Quall get himself killed before we know the significance of that, or our atoms won't be worth remembering."*

"Agreed," Uniss replied. *"But we have to fix this first."*

"Our list of options grows short, Uniss. You know Three has Starlin doing something despicable here. This world's karma axis is tilting ever negative, and H is just waiting for someone to make the critical error that will set him free. We must give this Quall direction or risk another Karmic Administration catastrophe."

"Yeah, I can feel it too, Dogg."

"Why don't we let the Quall recover his honor and help us at the same time? Then send him home to wait."

Uniss thought for a minute. He rubbed his face with one hand, and then finally nodded. "Okay."

Calmly, he placed his hat on his head and looked at Talaza. "Your target's karma score is a sad one, Blade Master. That means he is due to move on anyway."

Talaza looked from Uniss to Dogg. "What does that mean?" Talaza asked, not understanding.

"Well, it means," Uniss went on, "if you're swift, it just so happens we know where you'll find the individual who took your Analuke's life. His name is Bollard, Major Bollard. If you saw to it that he didn't make it back to Weirawind, we would be most grateful.

"Are you sure he's the one who took Analuke's life?" Talaza asked.

Uniss nodded. "He was the officer who led the Flaxon at that meeting and without warning took the first life."

"Not quite the order that things happened, what about the karmic flux?" Dogg asked via their mind link.

"A white lie," Uniss said. *"But it will serve the purpose and keep the balance."*

"So I have my target then?" Talaza asked.

"Consider it our request for a contract," Uniss said. "Payment is you get to deal with the Major as you see fit."

"Then, Star Lord, consider the target a walking ghost," Talaza said. "Point me and think no more of it."

Uniss watched Talaza pick up his knife belts and clip them in place, his actions deliberate and focused.

"He fled the battle and is moving through the pass as we speak," Uniss said. "By himself—I cannot say. Heading north, though. But with Major Bollard's death the vendetta ends, and Quall law is appeased, Blade Master. When it is done, return home. Say nothing of our meetings. Our paths will cross again."

Talaza nodded.

"Dogg will take you to the place," Uniss said. "After that it's up to you."

Talaza dipped his head in respect. Dogg trotted past him, leading the way.

"Come on, then, Blade Master," Dogg said. "Let's get you to where you need to be."

Without another word Talaza followed Dogg. Uniss watched as the pair descended into Yorr Pass to intercept their unsuspecting target.

*****

The night suited Talaza's eyes perfectly. Whilst Dogg had a coat that blended well with the night shadows, he could still easily follow her shape and wagging tail. Quall saw even better than the Scarzen at night. Though Talaza had not trodden this part of the mountain often, he still had firm knowledge of where he was on its treeless slopes.

With Dogg leading and being far more agile down the slope, it didn't take long for the gap between her and Talaza to widen. She finally stopped on a ledge overlooking the pass floor allowing Talaza to catch up.

Looking at him, Dogg said in a soft voice, "Below is the north entrance to Yorr Pass. See down there to the right? That soft light amongst the rocks?"

"I have it," Talaza whispered.

"That is the camp of a small Flaxon scouting party. No doubt Major Bollard should be approaching them very soon."

Talaza walked past her to take a better look and heard Dogg say; "None of the three down there must perish in your dealings with Major Bollard, understand?"

Talaza nodded.

"You may, however, incapacitate them."

Looking back over his shoulder, Talaza considered Dogg for a long moment. Makayass's earlier instructions suddenly struck him: *"Leave neither witness nor trace of your actions."*

"Hmm," Talaza said, "that is in conflict with my elder's instructions." He swung his view back toward the enemy camp, thinking.

"We have kept our side of the bargain, Blade Master," Dogg said, "as you are bound to keep yours."

Talaza turned to reply, but Dogg had vanished. Uneasily he scanned the rocky barren surroundings left and right. There was no sign of her. The wind picked up for a few moments and buffeted against his face. Then, a short distance away, he heard a voice with a malevolent tone muttering something. It sounded sinister and sent a shiver up his spine. A repulsive stench of rotting flesh crawled over him. As if the smell were a pushing hand, Talaza spun sharply and headed down the remainder of the craggy gray slope. Moving toward his target, his pace downward remained swift and silent. He saw no tomorrow or yesterday in his mind's eye, only now.

If Hex is displeased with me, he'll have to wait until my task is done.

His mind was haunted by images of his Analuke, who had been abandoned and left alone to die.

Soon Talaza's sharp ears caught the first fragments of conversation from the Flaxon camp below. Talaza checked for any sentries and saw none. He crept toward the camp and stopped next to a cluster of large fallen rocks that sat on the camp perimeter. There he peered around one of the boulders to see three seated Flaxon soldiers. The wind had dropped, which made it easy for the hardest of hearing to become suspicious about any strange noises. Talaza made his decision.

From a hollow leather rib on his shoulder, he withdrew a small blow tube made of cane. Then, from under a flap on his jacket, he took three small red bone darts. He crept closer to stand in the shadows between the natural split of two fallen boulders. There, he inserted the first dart into the pipe and raised the weapon to his lips. Aiming carefully, Talaza puffed a sharp breath. The dart sped across the space and struck the first soldier at the base of his jaw. The sting caused him to slap his face as if being stung by an insect. The other two chuckled at the soldier's groan and reaction. Moments later they found themselves doing the same thing.

The last one looked down at something in his hand. "Horse balls!" cried the soldier. "Hey! This ain't no bug! I been . . . struck."

The first soldier now looked pale and a moment later fell to the ground like a dropped wet sack of corn. The others stood and drew their long knives, looking for an enemy. From his position in the shadows, Talaza watched the first of the three convulsing on the ground.

"Arch! What's wrong?" said one of the two standing soldiers moving toward his fallen comrade. "Ah shak, what the—" Then he too collapsed in a heap and fell across his incapacitated ally.

The third soldier staggered two steps. "Come into the light, ya bushwackin' coward. Let . . . me . . . gi—" With a groan he too fell facedown into the dirt with a thud.

Talaza waited for the toxin to take full effect before entering the camp. Bodies cramping and catatonic, the three soldiers could only watch as Talaza approached. He was stronger than he looked, easily dragging each of the soldiers more than twice his own weight into position. He posed them around the camp against some rocks and a fallen stump as if they were dozing. He then ensured the fire looked freshly tended. One soldier still managed a throaty gurgle. So Talaza dragged him farther from the fire to the edge of the shadows and then stuck him with another immobilizing needle. From that distance, the soldier merely sounded like he was snoring.

"Good. Trap set. Now to wait," Talaza murmured.

Then he hid on the edge of the camp behind the fallen rocks.

***

It was near dawn by the time Talaza saw a lone mounted Flaxon enter the camp from the south. Both horse and rider looked exhausted and battered.

Applying his chameleon effect, Talaza felt the calm focus of a dispassionate lethal hunter fill his entire being. He saw the insignia of a ranking Flaxon officer on the soldier's uniform collar.

"Welcome, Major Bollard," Talaza muttered to himself.

"On your feet, you layabout!" Bollard ordered the first soldier to Talaza's right. "I could have killed you in your sleep."

The soldier said nothing, head lolling about, his body limp.

"In the name of the Regent, are you drunk, soldier?" Bollard demanded.

The soldier's eyes looked white with terror, but nothing spilled from his mouth except garbled drivel.

"You'll stand to attention when an officer speaks! I'll have you flogged if you don't respond—right now! When I find out who has been carrying brew on my field exercise, I promise you there'll be strife in his camp. On your feet—NOW!"

Bollard scowled at each of the men in turn. After getting no reaction from any of them, he prepared to dismount—but then paused to slap at his neck.

"Damn bugs!" he grumbled.

Talaza watched Bollard's eyes open wide as he looked down at his hand.

"You're no bug. You're a . . ."

His words faded, and Talaza looked on, knowing that Bollard's throat and tongue were now beginning to swell, with a fire spreading downward into his lungs. Holding his throat, Bollard gasped for air and slumped forward, falling from his saddle. He hit the ground shoulder first, the crushing impact snapping his clavicle. One hand on his throat and the other arm paralyzed, Bollard rolled onto his back, groaning in agony, and then tried desperately to sit up.

Talaza stepped from the shadows into the firelight, holding a straight blade in one hand. His heart burned with rage as he considered the executioner of his Analuke.

Barely holding a sitting position, Bollard's eyes turned toward Talaza, and he let out a strained cry. He desperately tried to reach inside his jacket for something, but his limbs failed to answer.

Intending absolute retribution, Talaza launched himself across the gap. Striking with all his might, he landed on Bollard driving a bone-shattering kick into Bollard's chest. The blunt force of the blow sent the major crashing onto his back.

Then the cramps and convulsion set in as the dart's toxin took hold. Clutching his devastated sternum, Bollard began to lose all control over his bodily functions. Dispassionately, Talaza watched the Flaxon officer writhe in agony. Slowly and deliberately, Talaza unwrapped his head coverings, revealing his milky pale-skin face, large eyes, and flat nose.

He knelt next to Bollard while the major convulsed in a spreading pool of his own filth.

Talaza looked pointedly at the other soldiers. "They felt the red dart," Talaza said in common tongue, waving a hand toward them. "All they'll have is a pounding stone-head and complaining stomach for quite some time when the effect wears off. But you . . ." Now Talaza looked down at Bollard. "You, Major Bollard, received the green dart. You are not so fortunate. You will linger awhile until everything inside stops working. Then you will ooze shak from every hole, praying to Hex for your end."

Talaza paused, watching as the realization of inescapable demise registered in Bollard's eyes.

"Look at me, Major Bollard. For what you have done to my Analuke, I allow you to see my true face. Consider this a parting gift. May Hex take your spirit and never let it rise again."

Talaza stared into the major's eyes. The dying Flaxon's contemptuous expression for his killer fell into disbelief.

A hint of desperation flickered in his eyes. *I'm an officer of the Regent's Court. How can Hex allow me to pass from this world in such squalor?"* Bollard's eyes glazed over and his head rolled to one side as he breathed his last.

✳✳✳

From a ledge above the Flaxon camp, Uniss and Dogg watched Talaza move around the camp preparing to leave.

"Think he'll be heading back?" Dogg asked.

"Yeah. Achieved what he wanted . . . and helped us too. I have him tagged now. He could be useful in the future. If either of us had to remove Bollard, that would have pinged Central's Karmic Register. And we don't need anyone from the Karmic Accounts Office coming for a look-see while we're trying to figure out just what Starlin is up to down here."

"You're right, but I wonder if any of what has passed in last hours really has anything to do with H—or Starlin for that matter? I mean, it could just have been a bunch of ordinary recarns living their lives and making random decisions. Nothing's like it once was. But my fur does tingle when the wind picks up here. Feels like one or both of them are looking over my shoulder, and then I wonder if it isn't just my paranoia for our present circumstance."

Uniss looked at her frowning. "A little paranoia is healthy right now after how we've been stitched up. Nah, it's them alright, one or both. They were always thick as thieves, even when Starlin marched our road. I'm certain of it, Dogg. He has a fingernail dug in everywhere."

"So now what?"

Uniss pushed the brim of his hat up and sighed. "Well, my feeling is we'll run in circles here until we have the new apprentice we've been lumbered with in the mix. At least if we look like we're toeing the party line, they'll give us enough breathing space to find out what Starlin's really up to. Three would just love to see us fail while he beats the system once again."

"I hear that, but how will a human cope in an environment like this?"

"By doing exactly as they are told or die tryin', just like we will if we don't get this figured out in time. A storm is rolling in, Dogg, and it's a granddaddy if ever I felt one."

"I know, and judging by what information wasn't handed over by Starlin's karma office about Ben, our new asset must be quite a firecracker."

Uniss nodded. "Agreed."

"Another human is an odd replacement. You know how the last one went."

"We still have the agent too, but that's different."

"Hmm, you're right. The agent retains free will; our apprentice is bound." Dogg's ears drooped. "Uniss, then that means a trip via ethereal mortal node and a time shift back to Earth."

"Yep. Sooner we have Ben Blochentackle on board and get back here, the sooner we'll straighten all this mess out. Hopefully we'll keep our atoms and our status as well."

Uniss looked around, considering final tasks, then said, "We have one last appointment in Weirawind City before we leave. You ready?"

"Do it."

With Dogg's last words, both raised their view skyward and the sound of a rushing electrostatic wind began. A glittering silver stream of light enveloped them. As it withdrew skyward, Uniss and Dogg vanished, bound for Weirawind City.

Act 3

CHAPTER

8

Unexpected Things

In the Flaxon camp, a sense of great suffering penetrated even the stones around Talaza. He looked around again, seeing each of Major Bollard's subordinates lying in agony, grasping their stomachs.

The major, dead as the stones around his corpse, had finished life lying in his own filth, as Talaza had predicted. It was a sign of just how lucky the others were. Talaza covered his face with his head wraps once more and then turned his focus to recovering Analuke's body.

Talaza folded his arms and thought for a moment.

Retracing my own steps back up the mountain to get to Analuke's last known position will take far too long. He looked to Major Bollard's mount still standing nearby. *But, retracing its plodding hoof prints, now that would take me swiftly to the very spot of the battle.* "Yes, that is the way."

Before he set off, Talaza dropped the saddles and bridles off the Flaxon mounts. He cut the hobbles and then scared the horses off in the general direction of the Flaxon border. After all, the horses had committed no crime. He then left the dead and the suffering to an uncertain future. Exposed to the elements and dangers this part of Ludd was known to contain, no rations for days and disorientation, Talaza knew their future wasn't bright. But it was a future nonetheless, unlike Major Bollard, who now no doubt was having to make account of himself in front of Hex. So, following the horse's earlier incoming trail, Talaza headed south into the treacherous natural corridor of cold stone, known as Yorr Pass.

***

Even though Talaza knew the pass well, its often twisting pathway and shadowed sheer cliff faces made him feel somehow imprisoned. By the time he'd made it a good third of the way in, moisture and gray fungus covered most rock faces on either side. Sunlight didn't have much influence here, even in the longer days of the hot season. The mortal and not so mortal dangers were well known here, forcing a lot of energy into keeping all his senses on high alert. Now and then, he thought he'd glimpsed movement ahead—or was it just the light? His ears played tricks too. Several times he was sure he heard the faintest unsettling whispers.

Most of the time, Yorr Pass was only traveled in the season of bud and bloom, when storm and winds were less frequent and days were longer. Sounds of rockslides or other nearby travelers carried farther then, giving plenty of warning. But this was the beginning of leaf-fall, a very different season. Any who used this passage accepted that chain-lightning storms and avalanches were a hazard during this time. Talaza looked skyward, hoping not to see any menacing weather. The sky looked unreachable like the perspective of an ant looking up through a funnel.

"Two-faced Flaxon," he muttered. "I should never have left Analuke. Stupid Talaza. I'll never ken the Flaxon ways for deceit."

Even though he moved swiftly, it still took some hours to cover the distance until finally the south exit of the pass presented itself. Keeping to the left shoulder of the approach, Talaza slowed, noticing rubble trickling to the ground just ahead of him. Cautious, he stopped and tried to see where the fall was coming from. Its origin disappeared in the upper shadows of the overhanging cliff face. Suddenly a cold dread enveloped him and a sinister nearby laugh seemed to emanate from all around. Then he heard a distant soft whistling from directly above.

A realization of imminent danger pushed him to dive away from the spot. He cried out in desperation, hitting the ground chest first in fear for his life. With a horrendous crash the many tons of a massive boulder struck the position he had just been standing in. The impact shook the ground around him, and the edge of the boulder's base pinned the toe of his right boot. With some effort he pulled his foot free and shuffled backward, wide-eyed in terror. Then, using hands and feet together, he scrambled away and rolled to a standing position.

"Well, the gods are smiling on you this night," said a familiar voice from behind.

Startled, Talaza turned away sharply from the natural death trap to see, Maleeka, Analuke's sister, looking at him. For a brief moment of hope, he thought the figure and voice belonged to Analuke. Seeing it wasn't, his head dropped in sadness and his heart sank.

"You should know better than to be using the pass at this time," Maleeka said. "I quite expected to walk right by you, unaware you were buried under a pile of slip stone, but you seem to like your death traps on a much larger scale."

Talaza looked back to the boulder and shrugged. "Well, I don't and I'm not. For a moment I thought you were—Where did you come from anyway? How did you find me?"

"Wasn't sure I could, but I had to try. After backtracking from the last place I saw Analuke and then visiting the site of the massacre, I followed a retreating horse's trail. Since there was only one set of Quall prints at the battle scene and no sign of you earlier, I began to search for markers. I knew you would leave them for her. I found one near the mouth of the pass and had just started in when I saw movement and heard the crash."

"Wait! The last place you saw Analuke? You mean not at the battle site? You saw her—alive? Where is she?"

"No, Talaza, I said I saw her—but not alive. She was being carried in the arms of a Scarzen warrior, who laid her to rest at the foot of Black Mountain near the message stones."

Talaza walked closer to Maleeka. "What did they do to her body?"

"Actually, from a distance anyway, I observed them giving her respectful last rites, I think."

"So, she is truly gone then."

Maleeka nodded.

Talaza's shoulders dropped.

"Yes, I'm sorry, Talaza. But I did recover this."

From a small satchel carried across her shoulder, Maleeka produced a length of Analuke's head wrap. Talaza recognized it immediately and took it from her. In the center of the strip of cloth, he saw the pendant he'd had given her on the day of their union. Talaza fought hard to hold the tears back.

Maleeka reached out to gently embrace him for a moment, then pulled back. "I'm sorry, Talaza. I recovered this once there were no threats to be seen. I observed another Scarzen do something similar for a fallen traveler a few seasons back. Only that was for a Celeron, who appeared to have been executed on the east boarder of Scarza. Their chest was full of Chou arrows. Anyway, to get closer to Analuke's position, I had to go around the blind side of a bluff to avoid being seen. But by the time I obtained a clear line of sight again, the Scarzen who had brought her there was gone. Someone else stood in their place, looking upon her body."

"Wait. What someone else? Another Scarzen?"

"Well, they were as tall as a Scarzen, only they were not wearing recognizable field armor like the common Scarzen warrior. This one had on an elegant purple robe, long and hooded, covering his face. I think he could have been the leader of the Scarzen Brasheer I encountered once."

Talaza's eyes opened wide. "The Brasheer!"

Maleeka nodded. "Yes. They seemed to be taking time considering something important while watching over Analuke."

"Take me there. I must go and see!"

Talaza turned to set off, but then he felt a hand on his shoulder.

"Wait!" Maleeka said. "Talaza, there is no point."

"No point?"

"There is nothing left to see. The one in purple robes gathered Analuke's body up in their arms and disappeared in a silver whirl of glittering light."

"Oh my. . ."

"When I went closer to look," Maleeka continued, "the only thing there besides that part of her head wrap were these orchids."

Maleeka reached inside her vest and withdrew a small fold of cloth. She unwrapped it and handed Talaza a delicate spray of budding white-and-purple stems.

"Scarzen revere orchids," Maleeka said gently.

"Yes, I know."

"These were at the spot I last saw Analuke's body."

Talaza took the orchids with tears welling in his eyes.

"Talaza." Maleeka stared at him. "We have now even more pressing matters."

Talaza looked up at her sharply. "Huh? What do you mean? What could be more important than paying my respects at the last known sighting of my heart's reason for beating?"

"Seeing to the welfare of your sons, for one thing. They'll need you now more than ever."

Talaza took a deep breath. "Yes, of course. But . . . what will I say to them?"

"You'll tell them their mother made a good account of herself kicking the enemy's backside into the next world. That would be a good start."

That's what Dogg said happened, Talaza remembered. He closed his eyes and hung his head.

"Talaza, hey!" Maleeka grabbed his arm. He opened his eyes and looked at her. "You need to focus, Talaza. There's more. Makayass has been taken by the Flaxon, and Tatute has been badly wounded in the attack as well."

"What? No!"

Maleeka gave a short nod. "Yes, just after you and Analuke left, Makayass and Tatute set off to join with the Grand Circle. While descending the east pass, they were ambushed by a company of Flaxon who tried to disguise themselves as Chou assault troops. Our entire escort was put to the sword, save one—Sorn. He was second officer on security detail. I was standing on the perimeter of our hamlet when I saw him stumbling toward me. He raised the alarm and then collapsed in my arms. With his last few breaths, he said the encounter was short and brutal and that Tatute was badly wounded in the exchange. His final words were that one Flaxon warrior in particular, whose coverings and headwear were all brown lead the assault. After killing our best with ease, the one in brown located Makayass and ripped him from his journey box by the throat. Sorn said he saw Makayass slash the one in brown with two of his poisoned hook blades, but they had no effect."

All brown? Talaza mused. A flush of concern and realization enveloped him, and he muttered, "Can this be the one the Star Lord warned of?"

"What?" Maleeka asked.

Talaza shook his head. "Nothing. How is this possible, Maleeka? Makayass's blades never fail to settle a contest in his favor."

"It happened, I can assure you. By the time we found the ambush site, the Flaxon and Makayass were long gone. Scouts said the trail dwindled to nothing near the Flaxon border. We found Tatute hiding in the underbrush and horribly injured. We have him back in the Longhouse now, and he is calling for you."

Talaza's shoulders slumped and he sighed. "I'm sorry for the loss of Sorn. He was a fine warrior, and someone important to clan line of succession should anything happen to Makayass. And I know he was personally important to you. Who is guiding the clan now?"

"That's just it. Wauk, who was Number One, and Sorn, who was Number Two, are both gone. Tatute directs that *you* must take the post to ensure stability within the clan."

"Me?"

Maleeka shrugged. "You were Number Three. You are now Number One. Congratulations, brother-by-law."

The expression in her eyes told Talaza she was genuinely smiling at him as she folded her top two arms.

"All your trying to stay in the background has come to naught," she said.

Talaza looked to the ground. "Guide the clan—me? Tatute must have been hit on the head very hard."

"No, listen, Talaza. This isn't a choice. You have the rank, respect, and age required. You have run the gauntlet and survived the death's gate three times. And you were born in the noble hour of the horned bat. You are now next in line, according to Cosa Clan law."

Talaza began pacing back and forth as his mind grappled with the implications of what he was being compelled to do.

"Yes," he said, halting his steps, "but I never imagined—"

"No, Talaza," Maleeka cut in, "neither did any of us, but there it is. You must return to take the seat until the life or loss of Makayass can be ascertained. No one kens the politics of the clans better than you. You know the infighting that will start if there isn't a firm set of hands holding us together very soon."

Talaza visible pulled back. "But my skills are best applied in the field, Maleeka. Ecknor is good at settling arguments. He is Tatute's apprentice. Let him sit in the debate circle."

Maleeka scoffed. "Ecknor would be poison in that position. You know the law. Clan leader of Black Mountain has to be a tested warrior and scholar in one. Ecknor is still using apprentice blades and has never been tested. The clan leader is called by our seer to assume the role. Tatute has called for you, Talaza, and *you* must answer that call. We also need a decisive plan to rescue Makayass, if he still lives and Ecknor has no such skill."

Talaza looked at her squarely. "Makayass does live, or you would have found his body amongst the dead too. As for a rescue plan in the midst of Flaxor's heartland, there is nothing quick to be done about such an excursion. Makayass was the obvious target of the ambush for the attack to be so focused."

Maleeka nodded. "See? A strategist through and through."

Talaza harrumphed and closed his eyes to think. His chest felt hollow and any strategy seemed hard to compose.

Finally he looked at Maleeka. "Very well. We'll return to Black Mountain. I will give the matter my full attention. The one in brown and all connected to the harming of Elder Makayass will be put down, and Makayass will be brought home, alive or otherwise. But when this is done, I will choose my own course. Ya ken?"

"Good enough."

With nothing more to say, they turned their attention toward home and set off for Black Mountain.

CHAPTER

9

Hard Choices

Talaza and Maleeka made good time back to Black Mountain, urged on by a steady wind and persistent rain. From the moment they set foot inside the hamlet's perimeter, a growing crowd followed Talaza as he lead them to the elder's Longhouse. Behind him Talaza could hear the buzz of clan voices asking Maleeka for answers: "Will Talaza lead us?" . . . "Does this mean Elder Makayass is dead?"

"Please," Maleeka said, frustration setting in. "Answers are coming."

"Who will avenge Makayass?"

Talaza came to a halt with his back to the crowd as Maleeka stepped up beside him. He heard so many footsteps shuffle to a stop close on his heels that the feeling of their sheer mass made him reluctant to turn around.

Maleeka touched him gently on the arm and leaned in to speak softly: "Before you go inside, you must say something. Give them something to carry on with."

When Talaza turned to face the crowd, he saw the entire population of Black Mountain staring back at him—including his two sons, Sooza and Cezarn who stood at the very front.

"Ahh . . ." Talaza began. "As you all know, a short time ago our mountain was assaulted. Many warriors gave their lives protecting Elder Makayass and Seer Tatute. We received a devastating blow with the attack on their caravan. It has hurt us deeply, but it has neither dealt us a fatal blow, nor broken our resolve to set things right. The brothers and sisters who fell in that assault will be avenged. The actions of those who had the audacity to attack us in our heartland will not go unpunished."

"Is Makayass lost?" asked someone in the crowd. "Who will lead us in his absence?"

"Seer Tatute has ordered Talaza to the post of Arbitrator until the matter can be sorted," Maleeka said.

Her statement drew a mixed reaction, eliciting a swell of voices until Talaza raised his two upper arms demanding their silence.

"Listen to me. Listen to me!" he ordered. "You all know that ending Elder Makayass is no easy task. He was alive by the last eyewitness account. When more is known, an announcement will be made. Meanwhile Seer Tatute has asked me assume temporary guardianship of the elder's seat."

"What do they want with him?" Sooza asked.

"We do not ken the reason for this brazen action—yet," Talaza said, then glanced around the crowd. "They are Flaxon, so likely ransom or extortion. For now this is uncertain. But what is certain is that Hex blessed us with the recovery of our beloved Tatute. His sight will guide us to bring Elder Makayass home safe and well. Please be patient and remain vigilant. It is not certain all the enemy have fled. Meanwhile sharpen your blades and take up your posts. Defend our mountain. Our border is now closed. I go into council with Seer Tatute to learn more and lay a plan to bring Elder Makayass home. Report any and all findings to the Longhouse Commander of the Watch. You will be called as necessary to aid in this mission." Talaza looked at his sons, then said, "Sooza, Cezarn, come."

Talaza turned and entered the Longhouse with Maleeka and his sons, leaving the crowd behind.

***

Inside the Longhouse the atmosphere felt subdued. Talaza could see Tatute at the far end, lying on a fur bed attended to by two carers.

"Maleeka, send a scout to advise the Grand Circle of the attack on our mountain," Talaza said. "Ensure they know Tatute is alive and well. Last thing we need right now is a coup from outside. Tell them Makayass could be only the first of many such kidnappings and to protect their own elders."

Maleeka bowed her head in respect. "As you wish," she said, then departed to see his order carried out.

Talaza looked to his sons who stood waiting for instruction just as three of the Black Mountain commanders, accompanied by Ecknor, entered the Longhouse and stood, clearly expecting an audience.

"Where is Mother?" Sooza asked holding Talaza's attention.

Talaza's mood softened at Sooza's question and he sighed. "My sons. Your mother is . . ." He took a deep breath and looked distractedly at the waiting commanders and then back to his sons. "There is a lot to discuss in private. Please allow me to speak with the commanders to ensure our home's safety. We will speak of it shortly, I promise. Stand to the back and remain silent while I and the commanders confer with Seer Tatute."

"Yes, Father," both answered with a bow of the head.

Talaza waved the commanders and Ecknor forward, and they all advanced toward the far end of the Longhouse where Tatute lay.

Ecknor walked up alongside Talaza and said, "This is a bit convenient, don't you think?"

Talaza paid Ecknor a cursory glance, but kept moving forward.

"You seem to have landed on your feet, Talaza," Ecknor said. "Just don't get too comfortable, Number Three. The firm ground beneath your feet can easily become sand if you don't enlist wise help."

Talaza shot Ecknor a cold glare. "And that wise help would be who—you?"

"Absolutely," Ecknor said, nodding.

Talaza came to a deliberate stop. He considered the distance from the apparently sleeping Tatute to them. Then he looked directly at Ecknor with the others looking on from behind, exchanging concerned glances.

Talaza spoke in a steady, flat tone: "You may be Tatute's second, Ecknor. You may even have his trust. But I have been called to answer for the clan until the matter of Elder Makayass is clear, and I take that post most seriously."

"Do you?"

"Yes, I do. And know this: I'll not tolerate your mischief a tip's worth of my blade while I have this responsibility. Dare to call my competency into question in front of the commanders again, and I'll have the Enforcer extract your entrails through your ears for slandering my honor. Ya ken?"

Talaza's confident posture and direct predatory stare told Ecknor that silence and compliance were his best reply. Ecknor bowed his head, showing respect, and then withdrew a full pace.

"Excellent," Talaza said. "Now, let's see if Tatute is up to conversing, shall we?"

The group approached Tatute and the two attendants caring for him. Talaza saw that the attendants had applied medicine and bandages to Tatute's lower right arm and left leg. Respectfully the group stopped and placed palms of their top two hands together. Tatute turned his head toward them and slowly opened his eyes.

"We are overjoyed you are returned to us safely, my master," Ecknor said.

Tatute looked from Ecknor to Talaza. "There is little time for pleasantries, Ecknor," Tatute said. "Talaza. Step closer."

Talaza did as requested, leaving Ecknor and his surprised expression behind.

"Closer, Talaza, come closer."

Talaza knelt in front of Tatute.

Tatute spoke in a weak voice: "I am sorry to learn Analuke has had her final battle. She will always be held high in our hearts. You know the jeopardy the clan is placed in?"

Talaza nodded.

"And that is why I need you to take the High Seat. This is, I know, what you were born to do."

"Elder Makayass will be returned to his rightful place, Seer, I vow it," Talaza said.

"Makayass now has an uncertain future," Tatute said. "We do not know where he is being kept or indeed if he is still alive. You must ascertain this to be one way or the other."

Talaza nodded again. "I will find him."

"No. The clan needs its leader here to keep the foundation strong. Choose someone you can trust to be your eyes. When you discover the truth, you report your findings directly to me."

Talaza shot the others a quick look and saw all of them watching his quiet exchange with Tatute intently.

Then Talaza looked back at Tatute. "I will do as you instruct, Seer."

"Good. Now let me speak to them."

Talaza moved to one side so Tatute could deliver his address.

"Let me be clear," Tatute said. "Until the truth of Elder Makayass's well-being is established, I have chosen Talaza to lead Black Mountain. You will inform your unit leaders that Talaza's word and direction are to be received as if they were the words of Makayass himself."

Talaza stood and the three commanders dropped to one knee, eyes down.

"As you instruct," they answered as one.

"Now," Tatute said, "take your seat at the other end of the Longhouse, Talaza the Elder. Bring resolution and sweet revenge to Black Mountain."

Talaza paid respect and turned to the others. "Join me at the High Seat," he said, and then made his way to the opposite end of the Longhouse.

A few paces behind, Talaza heard his sons whispering to each other.

"Why did the seer just call Father by that title? Is he elder now?" Cezarn asked.

"Shhh, brother. His post is in name only, for now, That's why Seer Tatute called him Talaza the Elder—not Elder Talaza. The temporary title is to ensure there isn't a coup in the absence of Elder Makayass. It stands until we see the body of Elder Makayass, living or dead."

Talaza came to a stop in front of the High Seat and turned to face the group. "Commanders, rally your squads. Prepare them for a battle most serious. We'll not be caught sleeping upright again. Ecknor, oversee a burning ceremony asking for Hex's blessing—one on the sunrise and one at dusk. Ensure you lead the devotions personally."

Talaza noted a flicker of discomfort cross Ecknor's eyes at having to take orders from him, but gave assent and bowed his head. "Now carry out your duty, I would speak to my sons in private," he said. "Sooza, Cezarn, join me."

Talaza felt for now at least that he had the commanders support and Ecknor's ambitious nature had been neutralized.

Now to a task most difficult, he thought. Stepping up onto the raised platform.

***

Sitting in the High Seat, Talaza looked upon his sons in front of him. He felt an unbearable weight settle upon his shoulders as they waited for him to speak. Mixed images and memories of Analuke and their time together swept passed his mind.

"We must speak of your mother now. What I will tell you is difficult, but I know she would want me to tell you the truth."

"She is passed, isn't she?" Sooza asked.

Talaza took a breath, then nodded. "Yes. There was an unpredicted turn of events during our mission in the Yorr Pass. She was caught in the middle of a skirmish between a Flaxon company and a Scarzen unit. She eliminated some significant enemies before she was cut down."

Both Sooza and Cezarn stood silent for a moment, eyes welling with tears.

Finally Sooza asked, "Where can we pay our respects? Where has she been laid to rest?"

Talaza felt a flush of anxiety of how to answer, then said, "It was observed that even the Scarzen paid your mother respects. She has been laid to rest in the forest of Yorr. When the matter of Elder Makayass's rescue is resolved, we will stand together to pay proper respects to her memory."

"Then what would you have us do in the meantime, collect spindling for the Longhouse fires?" Cezarn asked, a clear edge of anguish in his voice.

Talaza dropped his head as if he'd be struck by something blunt before looking up at his sons again. "No. In fact I have an important mission for you. One that will help reveal not only the kidnappers of Elder Makayass, but the culprits ultimately responsible for your mother's unpredicted demise."

"What are you talking about, Father?" Sooza asked.

Talaza looked about the Longhouse to ensure no unwanted eyes and ears were near by. He waved his sons to move closer. "My other two closest allies are dead. You are the only two I trust to report the truth to me. You will go to Weirawind City and locate Elder Makayass."

"Weirawind!" said Sooza in hard-pressed whisper. "Father, we have never been that far north. In fact Cezarn has barely left the foot of our mountain before. He has yet to even run the gauntlet for his coming of age."

"Don't argue with me, boy," Talaza snapped. "You're sounding just like your mother."

"Someone has to," Sooza said. "She isn't here anymore to be the voice of reason, is she? Leave Cezarn here, I will move faster and there will be less risk."

Talaza took a deep breath. "No. The mission calls for two and your brother has shown great potential in the stealth games. You will both be able to honor your mother by aiding me in this task. Your brother is as ready as he'll ever be, and I know you will look out for him. You have the instincts of a master tracker, Sooza. You have run the gauntlet with the best outcome since your grandfather assassinated the Celeron king's battle mage in Bon City. I need someone in the advanced party who will keep a cool head. Now can I depend on you or not?"

Sooza touched his brother on the shoulder, then said, "Yes, Father, we will not fail you."

"Good. We have little time and few options to work with to see this made right. I will supply you with the necessary maps to get you both to the city unhindered. Now here is the critical part: you'll discover the whereabouts of Elder Makayass first. You'll do this through observing the activities of Regent Trabonus who, I believe, is directly responsible."

"The regent!" Sooza said. "Father, that is an extreme target, a mission for one of the master infiltrators. He will be well guarded day and night."

Talaza nodded. "He is, I can assure you. Haven't you said for the last two seasons that you wanted to walk the path of infiltrator and bring highest honors to the clan?"

"Yes, but—"

"Then this is your chance. Your mother and I have visited Weirawind many times. We have several entry points where you can slip inside unnoticed. Once you have located and liberated Elder Makayass, if you can get close enough I also place a mark on Regent Trabonus."

Talaza could see by the eyes of his eldest son that his mind was racing.

"Kill or capture?" Sooza asked.

"You will confiscate his life without compassion or allow him any dignity in his passing. I want you to use Black Sky."

"Father, that is extreme!" Sooza said.

"No less than he deserves. I want his spirit bound to his body. Let them rot together with no chance of Hex's blessing. It will also keep the Flaxon healers guessing long after you are gone. The recipe is complex. Can you remember how to assemble his gift on the journey?"

Sooza nodded. "Yes. Provided I have Chorsa fish bones, I can gather the rest of the ingredients along the way."

"Ask Maleeka. She will have some. You may tell her alone what I have instructed you to do. Cezarn, you are to accompany your brother as his support. Sooza is in charge of the mission. Do exactly as he instructs."

"Yes, Father, thank you for the opportunity to avenge mother."

Talaza looked upon his youngest son with concern. "You are not going on a mission of revenge, Cezarn. You are going on a mission of recovery. Elder Makayass is your top priority. You'll need to skirt the Yorr Pass Neutral Zone. I'll mark the known Scarzen patrol routes. Stay off them. The last thing you need to be doing is evading a passing Scarzen patrol with a heavy load. Pack light for town engagement."

"Yes, Father," Cezarn said. "But I still only have one long knife, and I've not been sanctioned to have hunting blades."

"Oh . . . yes, I forgot. Well, I'll have to rectify that. Sooza, give Cezarn your blade belts."

"What? Father, these are some of the finest hunting blades on Black Mountain. You had them forged for me yourself."

Talaza nodded. "I did. That was for your coming of age rites. Now you have earned something better."

Reluctantly, Sooza took off his hunting blade belts and handed them to his younger brother, who accepted them most enthusiastically.

"Sooza," Talaza said, "in our yurt, under my bed, is a trunk."

"You mean Grandfather's trunk?"

Talaza nodded. "In it are his blade belts and long knives. There is also a throwing blade for each of you he had made before his passing two seasons ago.

The forger Attun crafted them for him. They were made with Scarzen red ore. I now make them *your* responsibility." Talaza eyes softened with pride. "Just don't cut yourself."

"Thank you, Father," Sooza said. "They will be used with good purpose. When do we leave?"

"Immediately. See to your final preparations and be on the road by dusk."

Sooza and Cezarn stood, paid Talaza due respect, and left the Longhouse.

As Talaza sat there alone, thinking on what must come next, the words of the Star Lord and his companion crossed his mind.

I wonder what they would make of all this.

***

Sooza and Cezarn went to the communal food storage hut and asked for some light rations to go on a short hunting trip down the mountain. The moment they exited the rations hut, they came to a stop upon being confronted by Ecknor.

"And where might you two be running off to? Where are you being sent?" Ecknor asked.

Caught by surprise, Sooza stood looking at Tatute's apprentice, trying to think how to legitimately send him on his way. "Well, Seer, we . . . uh——"

Just then a scout came running up to them interrupting Ecknor's grilling: "Sooza! Do you know where your father—I mean, Elder Talaza—is? I have an urgent message from the commander on the perimeter."

Sooza looked from Ecknor to the scout. "Uh . . . yes, here, follow us. We'll take you to him. Forgive me, Seer. Urgent matter to attend to."

Using the opportunity to escape the interrogation, Sooza and Cezarn led the scout to the Longhouse and ushered them inside.

***

As Talaza saw his sons hurrying toward him with a scout, his concern for a worsening situation climbed. The puffing scout, followed closely by Sooza and Cezarn, stopped short in front of Talaza, and all three paid respect.

"What's all this then?" Talaza asked.

"Elder," Sooza said, "this scout has an urgent message and asked to be brought to you right away."

The scout stepped forward. "Elder Talaza. Commander Toonute of Perimeter Security asks this note be put in your hands immediately."

Talaza took the note from the scout and dismissed him.

"We will leave you to your work," Sooza said, paying respects and backing away.

Talaza nodded, still reading the note the scout had presented. Suddenly, he looked up for his sons who were now stepping toward the door.

"Wait," Talaza called. "Back here to me."

"What is wrong?" Sooza asked as they strode back toward Talaza.

"This is a ransom note. One demanding something—something most difficult."

"What is it?" Sooza asked.

"We now know that Makayass is in the custody of the Flaxon regent, Trabonus." Talaza shook the note at them briefly before referring back to it.

"His demands are that if we ever want to see Elder Makayass again, we will recover the personal journal of a Celeron alchemist called Ereedaa."

"That doesn't sound like such a difficult job," Cezarn said. "Where is this journal? We'll retrieve it straightaway."

Talaza looked up from the note and stared off to the far wall, then exhaled an exasperated breath. "Do not speak so fast about what you do not understand, Cezarn. Talon East. The journal is in the Scarzen bunker of Talon East."

"A Scarzen bunker!" Sooza said. "How will we even recognize such a journal?"

Talaza examined the note again. "The note says . . ." He muttered to himself, reading carefully. "Look for Ereedaa's red seal on a blue-wrapped volume that he carries everywhere."

"What would a Celeron be studying inside a Scarzen bunker?" Sooza asked.

"Well . . . the things most of interest to an alchemist are to do with changing one substance into another." Talaza thought for a moment and then it dawned on him. "Oh, shak! The one thing Scarzen value above all else is their blue crystal."

Talaza looked to both of his sons. "To be found with anything relating to that in your possession is an act of war on Scarza itself," Talaza said. "That's a death sentence all on its own."

Talaza looked back to the note. "The assassination of alchemist Ereedaa is to be carried out when his journal is taken. Attempting that on their home ground is another act of war and an insult to their ability to protect their own. If we are caught, it will bring the wrath of all Scarza upon the whole Quall nation until we are dust. We have three days to do this task. We must provide proof of our success to a Flaxon unit commander camped in the Yorr Forest by the end of the third day. Failure means they publicly execute Elder Makayass."

"So we are not going to Weirawind City?" Sooza asked. "We are now going south instead? Wouldn't going to Weirawind to find and rescue the elder be easier than infiltrating a Scarzen bunker?"

Talaza glared at his ignorant son. He walked up to them in frustration.

"Don't you see?" Talaza said. "There is no guarantee that Makayass is even in Weirawind. We must see the ransom instruction through. And then there is the issue of repercussion on the part of the Scarzen. Even if you are successful, that equals humiliation for the Scarzen on their home ground. They will not rest until the scale is equal again. We are caught between two enemies. Besides, in all our history the result is always the same where a Scarzen bunker is concerned: two go in, one comes back."

"What does that mean?" Sooza asked.

"That is the typical loss for any mission into a Scarzen bunker. Two go in, one comes back. That's how we lost your uncle Perta, and he was the best stealth warrior we'd ever seen. They sent his head back in a bag and left it at the bottom of Black Mountain Pass with a note that said: *Next time we come to you.*"

Sooza nodded. "I was young, but I remember."

"And never forget it!" Talaza snapped. "Their bunker's streets can change day or night. There are traps everywhere to end an ignorant intruder's wanderings most painfully."

"The moving walls you've spoken about are what concern me most," Sooza said.

"Yes, they can turn a long passage into a short one or cut two ends off to make the middle a kill zone. No way out. If you are detected in there, you die. The patrols inside the walls are never predictable and their stealth is equal to our own. They never speak openly to give commands. You don't just sneak into a Scarzen bunker unnoticed, grab what you came for, and slip out a window. Certainly not without many days of observation and planning."

"You and Mom did it," Cezarn said.

"Yes, and near lost our lives every time. By Hex's eyes, boy!" He shook his head. *Maybe this is a mistake.* "To try such a mission in just two days means you'll be shaking hands with Hex well before you're due. This requires time, and planning, both of which are in very short supply. It's almost as if they know it's impossible and want us to fail in plain sight."

"What choice do we have?" Sooza asked. "Elder Makayass is depending on us. I know my way across the Neutral Zone. My gauntlet was conducted there. We have listened well to your stories ofthe bunkers and the city of Weirawind too. We know it's a mission of some risk, but we are up to the task. We have learned our craft well and will evade their eyes easily at every turn."

Talaza grunted to himself. "Oh, son, your words make the reality of entering a bunker sound so much like a training drill of little consequence. It is not. A Scarzen doesn't have to see you to know you are there. They have many detection skills and ruthless ways to nullify their quarry. Seers such as Tatute say they can even hear each other's thoughts from some distance. They exist for just such a challenge, my son. You can never take their apparent actions as the mark of their true aim."

"We must try, Father," Cezarn said.

"Yes," Sooza said. "For the sake of our clan if for nothing else. You can advise us on what to look for and how to enter and leave their labyrinth undetected."

Talaza shook his head. "There is no negotiating with a Zukaa bull's horns if it finds you amidst its herd. The smallest mistake and . . ." Talaza took a breath. "No. There must be another way."

Sooza stepped up and touched Talaza on the arm. "Father. If we do not do this, then Elder Makayass is lost for certain. And with the note seen by the other commander, in the aftermath you could be judged harshly for not doing all you could have. Some, like Ecknor, would twist it and say you seized the opportunity to take the High Seat for yourself."

Talaza looked at his son. "I just lost your mother. I don't want to lose you both too."

"We all lost dearly in this, Father," Sooza said. "You must protect Cosa Clan. You must trust us to help you do that."

Talaza held his eldest son's gaze. "Your mother put a better head of reason on your shoulders than I seem to carry, didn't she?"

"And it's your influence that shows us the way forward. This is a real way we can honor her memory, Father. Please."

Talaza held off answering for a long moment, then said, "Alright, alright. Do as you must."

"We will not fail you, Father," Sooza said."

"You are your mother's sons, I'll give you that. Gather your things. I will tell you what I can and also send Maleeka with you as far as the walls of Talon East. And then you're on your own, after that I need her back here. Ecknor is clearly up to something, but I have no proof. I need Maleeka to keep him distracted. May Hex bless you in your efforts and bring you home safe."

CHAPTER

10

Unknown Enemies

As per Talaza's instruction, and being careful to keep an eye out for Ecknor, Sooza collected his grandfather's blade belts from their family yurt. It was just before midday when the brothers left Black Mountain settlement, heading for the south-facing descent. Maleeka was already there waiting for them as they approached. She was clearly kitted out for a journey involving much violence: blade belts crossing her chest, a short hunting bow over one shoulder, and a travel satchel slung on the other. Aside from those items, another small satchel was slung diagonally from one shoulder to her hip.

"You have everything you need for a hazardous journey, I hope?" she asked her approaching nephews. "Water skin, travel rations, flint and striker, sharpening stone, clean underwear?"

"Ha-ha, very funny," Sooza said. "Yes, Pra Maleeka we have everything."

Sooza and Cezarn both rolled a shoulder forward to show the two carry bags all Quall used for such a journey.

"Good. Won't be back this way in a hurry," Maleeka said. "And where did you get those blade belts from, Sooza? Haven't you been maintaining your kit? Your brother at least looks like his kit is properly respected."

Sooza looked at his brother and then the immaculate blade belts he himself had always maintained so meticulously.

Cezarn pushed his chest out with pride. "They are always given due attention daily, Pra Maleeka, just as instructed." He winked at his brother.

"Good to see," Maleeka said. "As for your kit, Sooza, you could take a leaf out of your younger brother's book. With the grime and shak your belts are covered in, looks like you found them in your grandfather's war chest. Dirt like that will make a blade stick in the scabbard in the cold of leaf-fall and the season of White, don't you know."

"Uh. . . Yes, I know, and I did," said Sooza, proudly patting the dust-covered blade belts crisscrossing his warrior's vest proudly. "Father wanted me to have something befitting the mission."

Maleeka cocked her head to the side. "Oh, now I see, yes. Well, he might have looked in the war chest first to see exactly what he was passing on." She examined Sooza's blade belts closer. "Yes, that's them alright. I am surprised Talaza let you have them. Finest Quall metal ever poured and folded went into them. Make sure you pay them due respect the moment we set camp. Bring them up to a hunter's standard, ya ken?"

Sooza nodded. "Yes, Pra Maleeka."

"I may be your pra, but this is a real mission. None should know our ties. It's leverage in the event of capture, ya ken? So 'Maleeka' will do fine."

"Yes . . . Maleeka," Sooza said awkwardly.

"I'm ready too, Maleeka," said Cezarn, preening the immaculate blade belts his brother had passed on.

"Since your father had little time to prepare you, my task is to accompany you to the walls of Talon East. I'll educate you as to what we know about it on the way. Then I must return to Black Mountain. Your father is well liked, but there are those who are scheming, whose intentions are not consistent with his and our hamlet's welfare, ya ken?"

"Yes, we do," Sooza said.

"Then let's get to it. The pace will be brisk. We aim to set first camp at the Lyran Gates. See there, in the far distance?" Maleeka pointed to the southeast of the mountain range. "We have to be there by the mid of night."

There, in the direction Maleeka indicated, the brothers saw a natural break in the range that gave access to the southern regions of the Ludd continent.

"Now," Maleeka said, "down the pass here and mind your step."

The three set off, with Maleeka in front and Sooza bringing up the rear.

***

Their view down from the steep path looked upon a wide forested valley stretching away west as far as their eyes could see. It was a natural corridor of land between the Lyran Mountain Range in the south, Black Mountain in the northeast, and mountains Trilix Di and Trilix Tian to the northwest. The valley's gently rolling hills sheltered the one meandering stream bringing water to the region, giving a misleading appearance of tranquility.

"It's good the practice runs are over," said Sooza, trying to be dry in humor while following in the other two's footsteps.

"You never liked practice," Cezarn said.

"There is nothing about what you're doing here that resembles a drill," Maleeka said. "After this you'll either be honored by the elder and given a yurt of your own in recognition. Or, you'll both be dead and an honor fire burned in your names for one full pass of the moons. Your blade belts will then be hung high in the Longhouse and your names will be heard in song while you take your place with Hex. I'd aim for the former. Keep moving. We'll be hard pressed to get to camp one on time."

Sooza always loved the air in this part of the Black Mountain's descent. The breeze smelled clean, and small glowing fungus flowers were a treat for the eyes, even in daylight. As they drew closer to the tree canopy below, a multitude of birdlife could be seen in the treetops.

"Hey, Sooza," said Cezarn, looking over his shoulder. "Do you think the panthera pride is still active down there? Maybe after the mission, we can do some tracking, find a den, and bring back some furs."

"We are heading on to infiltrate a Scarzen-filled bunker," Sooza said. "I'm sure they will be predator enough for us.

"Agreed," Maleeka said. "Keep your mind on the job, Cezarn. We are near the bottom of the pass. It is very possible that we'll encounter travelers and trappers from here on."

***

With the heavy trekking of the descent behind them, the three Quall passed beyond the main forest line on the Neutral Zone valley floor. Under the canopy, dappled sunlight illuminated the vegetation. The temperature was noticeably warmer unlike the windswept mountainside. Wildlife paths of various widths riddled this part of the forest.

Maleeka tested Sooza and Cezarn's knowledge of the landmarks while using them to keep their direction steady.

"How do the Scarzen navigate the Neutral Zone, Maleeka?" Sooza asked. "What was your first encounter with them like?"

"It is uncertain, but observation of their movements suggests they use some of the same landmarks we do. Things like that large spread of Koidzumii Bush over there, to the right," she said, pointing. "I saw part of a Scarzen map once that confirmed as much. This spread has been here for generations. We call it the Bleeding Hooks. You'll see what I mean when we get closer."

In the mid-distance the tall, formidably barbed natural hazard formed an impenetrable wall to the south for some way.

"We should navigate around it for now," Maleeka said.

"Yes, I think I remember Father speaking of it before," Sooza said.

"I bet he did. He got lost in there for two days once trying to take the shortcut. As for my first encounter with the Scarzen, let's just say I never made the same mistake twice."

A few more steps in the direction of the Bleeding Hooks and Maleeka's advance suddenly stopped. She made a firm hand sign of a raised fist for them to stop and stay silent. They all crouched low. Sooza looked ahead for any sign of threat, but saw none. Maleeka gestured for them to take cover quickly to the right. They headed low to a large moss-covered fallen tree trunk that had a thin veil of underbrush covering one side. Maleeka made sure she positioned herself between the brothers.

What is it? Sooza wondered.

He looked about for the danger. The birds still sang. Nothing seemed out of the ordinary. Then Maleeka's intense focus on something up ahead told Sooza different.

"Something coming," she whispered.

Some moments passed, still with no apparent sign of threat, and then Maleeka made a hand sign pointing to figures emerging from the underbrush. Sooza and Cezarn followed her indication with their eyes. With barely any warning and almost no noise, a Scarzen patrol of five suddenly came into plain view as though they had discarded some cloak of invisibility. Sooza and particularly Cezarn, felt a cold flush of apprehension for their first real encounter with the warriors of Scarza. Sooza felt Cezarn begin to move.

"Stay down!" ordered Maleeka in an intense whisper. "Quickly, use your chameleon skill and hold it until I tell you to release it."

Focusing internally, each of the Quall's skin and coverings took on the dappled color and hue of the rough bark and underbrush around them. In a few short seconds their transformation had made them almost impossible to see. They watched the Scarzen patrol approach, shifting its bearing toward them and the near side of their cover.

"Don't move a muscle," Maleeka said softly.

Watching the Scarzen, Sooza saw no sign of command or gesture as the unit of five adjusted their advance. If the one in the center shifted in any direction, the others compensated immediately without even looking at him. They seemed to be searching for something. As they approached, however, the Scarzen paid no attention to the Quall's position.

What now? Sooza wondered. He looked for any alternative cover. *Nowhere else to run from here.*

Sooza felt a crawling insect run up over his head—to keep on going, he hoped. He wanted to touch his head to check and fought hard to resist the impulse. He tried to distract himself, remembering his father's campfire descriptions of the power that a Scarzen battle circle wielded. How they used their will in coordinated fury to destroy their enemies. How they used a mysterious spirit energy Talaza said Tatute called "kin."

How will we fight against such a thing? Sooza mused.

As the front two warriors of the unit passed by their position, the details of their armor and weapons became very clear to him.

Shak! Sooza thought. *They're much bigger in real life.*

Each wore thick, dark drommal-hide armor, covering them neck to ankles. Heavy black slaa-thread and hide boots covered their feet. Sooza thought all the Kurjas' uncovered faces looked permanently angry, like they'd bite your head off just for being close by. One of the passing warriors turned momentarily in their direction. Sooza recognized the insignia of Talon East Bunker embossed into his leather cuirass—a gold-leaf tree over crossed war axes. It was just as the storytellers had described in the Story Hut back home.

What are they searching for out here? Sooza wondered.

Each warrior carried a melee weapon in one hand. One had a straight blade; another carried a curious double-headed short axe. The warrior in the center—the commander, Sooza figured—was even more conspicuous. He carried no obvious weapons at all. Instead his arms hung by his sides, with the palms of his hands open and facing forward.

The Quall sat stone still as the unit passed right by their position. Maleeka sat calm with the familiarity of being in such situations. She felt confident in Sooza's grit; but she couldn't say the same for the younger Cezarn. He'd still not been tested for exposure to the real-world pressures of Quall battlefield life.

Just when the Scarzen in the center of the patrol seemed on an easy course to pass by them, he stopped. With the small breeze blowing in the Quall's direction, their keen sense of smell detected the distinct Scarzen body odor: strong red tea and curry spice. Talaza had introduced his sons to it by providing samples of Scarzen personal articles collected from missions. With that smell came rule one of fighting Scarzen: keep to the shadows.

"Close enough to smell them is close enough to die before you can lift a blade."

Sooza watched the Scarzen commander turn slowly this way and that, fluttering his hands.

What's he feeling for? Sooza wondered.

The Scarzen seemed to relax for a moment and so too did the Quall. Then the unarmed Scarzen showed his true power. Arms still by his sides, he began releasing random energy pulses from open hands. The bolts of silver-white sizzling energy shot through the air, striking tree trunks near and around them. The impacts gouged large holes in the timber, spraying wood splinter everywhere, including over Sooza and the other two. Energy shocks scattered the birds in the trees above and sent small wildlife scurrying for cover in the underbrush. Maleeka didn't move, she understood what was happening, Sooza held fast too. But Sooza felt his brother's apprehension.

He's going to break, Sooza thought.

Still watching the Scarzen commander, from the corner of his eye, Sooza saw Maleeka carefully reach for Cezarn with her closest hand. Latching onto one of Cezarn's arms, she held him in place. To run now meant they'd be dead before they took three steps from cover.

Cezarn squirmed a little in Maleeka's grip, as the closest Scarzen turned in their direction, looking about and sniffing the air. The Scarzen stared directly at their position, and for the first time in his life Sooza felt his blood truly run cold. The Scarzen made a gesture to the others to the right of the Quall's cover. He then shot another bolt of that energy into the underbrush. A large tuskaboar squealed and charged forward, straight toward the Scarzen carrying the double-headed axe. Sooza guessed the shoulder of the muscular beast would easily reach his sternum. Shrieking and wailing, the wild mammal used a desperate burst of speed to try and evade the advancing Scarzen warrior, who'd deliberately barred its way. It seemed to Sooza that, for a brief moment, the animal had made its escape. That was until the Scarzen's axe-wielding hand flung the weapon horizontally at the fleeing beast. The spinning axe's trajectory intersected precisely with the tuskaboar's escape path. The axe struck deep into the neck of the animal, causing it to nosedive and tumble tail over head to the ground, killing it instantly.

Holding their nerve the Quall watched the tall Scarzen walk over to the dead animal. Sooza wondered what would come next. The Scarzen removed his axe with a deft yank of the handle, and then picked up the kill by one back leg. He held it aloft like he'd won something.

The Scarzen commander nodded and said something unintelligible. One of the other Scarzen warriors jogged over to assist. The two took little time to section and sack the back legs, neck, and forequarters of the beast. Then the commanding warrior walked on and the rest of the unit followed his lead. In the mid-distance Sooza, Maleeka and Cezarn watched the unit close ranks. Then, simultaneously, their images became blurry and they seemed to just blend in with the rest of the forest. The three Quall breathed a sigh of relief to see them gone.

"Mother's eyes!" Sooza whispered, still watching and partly expecting the Scarzen to reappear. "That wasn't how I thought my first contact with that Kurja clan would be."

Cezarn went to move from cover, but Maleeka gripped his arm even tighter, holding him fast.

"In Hex's name, when I tell you to stay put, you deng well stay put, ya ken!" She looked at her young nephew her eyes clearly displeased with him. "Getting yourself killed is one thing. Getting us killed before the mission is even underway is a disgrace. At this rate you won't last long enough in this land to have even a single story to be remembered by!"

"I'm sorry, Pra," Cezarn said. "I—"

"Don't 'sorry' me! If you had moved a head nod more, we were all going to die just now!"

Cezarn nodded, then said, "I thought we were discovered."

"I know you did," Maleeka said, "but that is their game. Learn it—learn it well. They were hunting for dinner. Thanks to your disregard for orders, you almost made it us!" She rose and walked away a few paces. "Do that again out here and I will bleed you dry myself, ya ken."

"Yes, Maleeka."

"Keeping your resolve in a tight spot will often be all that's between you and being served up from a Scarzen's campfire pot with hot spice and tates."

Neither of the brothers had ever seen this hard side of their pra before. She'd always seemed so tolerant and easygoing, but they'd heard whispers of her ruthless reputation in the field. This was the first time, however, any such venom from her had been directed their way.

"Scarzen don't really eat their enemies . . . do they?" Sooza asked, beginning to wonder.

Maleeka looked at him. "Maybe not. But it won't stop them from enjoying the exercise of cutting off your arms and legs for a lark and then throw you into the fire pit. Now let's go. We're heading in the opposite direction of that unit, thank Hex. We shouldn't see them again with a bit of luck. We still have a long march to first camp. The closer we get to the Lyran Gates, the higher the likelihood of running into a Scarzen patrol. You never know your luck in the Neutral Zone, as you just experienced, so stay sharp."

∗∗∗

With that small taste of "Meet the Scarzen" out of the way, the three proceeded southwest. The mountainous shoulders of the Lyran Gates now began to dominate the horizon. They followed the barrier of koidzumii bush for some time to find a way around, but it wasn't long before the forest undergrowth became impassable. Maleeka stopped to get her bearings.

"I thought the koidzumii would have thinned out by now," she said. "This part of the Neutral Zone changes so quickly, though."

"Looks like this plant is taking over the forest here," Sooza said, pointing. "There are mounds and hedges of it everywhere, some of it nearly as tall as the Scarzen. How do they get around it? Father told us it was thicker up this way on his last trek—do you remember, Cezarn?"

"Yes, it was mentioned in the stories last moons," Cezarn said.

Sooza nodded. "Father said there is a way through if you read all the signs right, if I remember correctly."

"He also said that if you don't, it's easy to get lost in there for good," Cezarn said. "Uncle Tadant says Scarzen bury their treasure in koidzumii."

Maleeka snorted a quiet laugh. "Your uncle says a lot of things, he's a storyteller after all. He's also old and smokes far too much dream moss in the Story Hut. Only thing I've seen Scarzen do with koidzumii is set fire to it to clear ground in their slaa worm groves. But I did find evidence of using it for rope-making once. For good reason, a cluster like this we call a 'shredder labyrinth.'"

"Is it really as nasty as it looks?" Cezarn asked.

"You'll see," she said. "We can't waste more time heading this way. We are going to have to go through."

"Through!" Sooza blurted.

"Yes, through," Maleeka said. "You got a problem with that, we can turn around for Black Mountain now. I'll tell your father that the mission was just too big a challenge."

"What? No! We can do this, right, Cezarn?"

"I never said we should turn back."

"Then watch the spines," Maleeka said. "They'll gore you deep. In your great-grandfather's day, they were used to tip the heads of spears and fishing arrows."

Maleeka found a narrow navigable corridor through the mushroomed mounds of interlocking spines. She led the way in.

"Keep your hands inside the path at all times and my stepping rhythm in your feet," Maleeka said. "Keep one eye on me, and the other on the Lyran Gates on your horizon."

The animal trail snaked its way through the labyrinth, often turning a blind corner. Sooza and Cezarn quickly found that, razor-sharp thorns or not, Maleeka set an unexpectedly fast pace. Following in her footsteps, they just had space enough to put a firm boot down where her foot in front had lifted off. In no time at all, it became apparent to Sooza why it would be so easy to get lost in a koidzumii labyrinth. Squiggling off in all directions, the path constantly broke away at junctions that only animals would know the reason why. Often they heard small creatures scurrying about through the thorn-filled underbrush.

These would be speedy pathways for one low and on four legs, Sooza thought.

Once they'd settled into a steady rhythm, the biggest test of the brother's attention was the monotony of the endless rolling thorn-scape. A substantial way in, Maleeka told them that the reason most of the tracks were so well trodden was because they served as tuskaboar thoroughfares.

Great—trampled and cut to pieces before we even get close, Sooza thought.

Later, one small error in an uneven step caused Cezarn to stumble, and the unforgiving thorns punctured his outstretched gloved hand with ease. The needle broke off in his upper left hand, causing it to throb and ache badly.

"We'll have to get that out before you get flesh swell," Maleeka said, stopping at the next junction.

Having to stop to remove the poisonous half-inch needle head before it infected the hand took precious time. Maleeka cut the barbed thorn out using one of her fine quiet-kill blades. She then pulled a fold of material from her satchel containing balm made from squirk climber fat and applied some to the injury.

"That should do it," Maleeka said. "Tell me if the throbbing doesn't die down in a short while."

"If it doesn't?" Sooza asked.

"Then we might have to remove the hand before the flesh swell spreads into his upper arm."

Her nephews looked at her horrified.

She coughed a small laugh. "Only joking. You'll be fine. How many three-armed Quall have you seen running about the place anyway?"

"Um, a couple," Cezarn said. "Pra Helka and Hunter Muggas. He has one hand and two fingers on another missing and—"

Maleeka shook her head. "Muggas doesn't count. Lost his bits fighting off a jaw fish when he was trying to swim the North River gap to eliminate a Chou official. Still accomplished his mission too, I might add. Pra Helka was born that way. You shouldn't ever ask her about it. She can get aggressive."

"Then what about Hunter Lutisha from Tarsh Clan in the west who comes to trade?" Sooza asked.

"Yes, right. Well, a Quall's life has its hazards," said Maleeka, doing up the strap on her satchel. "We should get moving. There is only a short way to go now and we'll be on the other side."

***

Maleeka had indeed been correct. A few more blind turns and the three exited into a small clearing on the other side of the Bleeding Hooks. Here the forest grasses were tall and pale, and the tree canopy thinner. They could see the steady gradient of the foothills leading to the Lyran Gates in the distance. A forest corridor showed the way to their destination. The shortcut had saved them considerable time.

"We'll stay within this tree line and use the shadows for cover," said Maleeka. "Gantry Town is not far to the south from here. We must we mindful of patrols and some of the strange travelers that frequent that place."

Maleeka strode forward, leading them on.

"Are there many Kurja at Gantry Town?" Sooza asked. "All the stories say it has been there for all the memory of the clans. How can that be? And who settled the town? Was it Flaxon or Chou? And why is there never a mission to Gantry Town?"

"Neither. Gantry Town is not like other places, Sooza. It has mischief of its own. Anyone may go there in the open, even the Quall. But no contract may be bought or served by any clan there . . . if they ever wish to be seen again outside of its walls."

"How long till we set camp?" Cezarn asked. "My hand is still not feeling so great."

"We've made good time," Maleeka said. "We'll be there by nightfall. Time to put some ground behind us. Come on."

Through the thinning forest line, Maleeka picked up the pace. For a long time their feet struck ground with a steady intense rhythm. The Lyran Gates now stood clear—imposing and within reach. Breaking free of the forest for the ascent, Sooza and Cezarn found keeping up with their pra was no easy task. Though accustomed to long treks, the unsteady and sometimes treacherous terrain took all their focus. There were many natural hazards, including bottomless gray shale pits.

"We make camp there," said Maleeka, pointing to the belly of the ginormous gap. "Talon East is on the other side. We are exposed here and the cold will set in soon, so keep moving."

A leftover core of an ancient volcano stood as a mountainous pillar of rock on the gates' left. It formed one shoulder of the natural U-shape that could be seen for many leagues on either side of the range. Now low in the sky, the late-day's sunlight had an uncommon green-orange hue to it. Sooza began to feel that the growing shadows too had an unnatural menace to them.

It was on true dark by the time they topped the rise to the camp Maleeka had chosen. By that time the brothers were ready to sleep where they stood. The last while had seen them begin to lag behind their pra. They looked forward to putting their load down, hopefully a drink, something to eat, and a seat at a campfire, even if it just offered the comfort of firelight. The sky was clear this night, so there'd be no chill of rain to fight against, thank Hex.

Sooza saw that Maleeka had stopped just up ahead near the edge of something. He placed a hand on his brother's shoulder.

"Come on," Sooza said. "Our legs can't fail here."

The flat shelf of stone and earth that greeted them was outlined by a black lip on the far side that met the horizon. The full moons of the round, along with their eyes now well adapted to night, allowed most details of the place to be clear. Here and there deep shadows hung around small clumps of trees. Uneven blades of stone jutted out from the main mass on their right, like monstrous mushrooms sprouting from a huge trunk. Away from that edge Sooza noticed another possible approach farther on that faded into shadow.

"Come," said Maleeka quietly, waving them forward. "Come see."

What Sooza and Cezarn saw when they walked up to stand beside her took their breath away.

"Welcome to Talon East," she said.

"Hex's eyes, it's . . . it's so vast," Cezarn said.

"Is it built straight into the side of the mountain?" Sooza asked.

"All Scarzen bunkers are," Maleeka said. "You could fit twelve of our Black Mountain settlements, including crops, in one quarter of that place and still have room. All of them made of solid black stone. This one has been in our stories from the beginning. The others are of the same design."

The shape of the bunker amounted to something of a sprawling rectangle. Its defense walls, even from here, looked a formidable challenge to access. The sound of a great horn resonated in the far distance.

"I know that sound.. Is that. . ." Sooza recalled a conversation with his father about bunker operations. Then he remembered Talaza having a lark with Analuke. Sooza almost laughed out loud. A picture of his father blowing into a large hollowed out stendle branch came to mind.

"That signals a change of guard somewhere inside," Maleeka said. "It's the only thing we can say is predictable behind those walls."

Now and then the small twinkle of lights seen indicated possible structures and perhaps street torches that sat against the ink of night. Sooza could pick out thumbnail lines of hundreds of stone buildings with flat rooftops interspersed with vegetation. It stimulated Sooza's tired head to wondering about their way in.

"It looks impregnable," Sooza said.

"To all but an elite few, it is," Maleeka said. She gently touched Sooza on the shoulder. "I know what you're thinking, but you'll think it better once we set camp and get some food in your belly. Over there, against that wall under the ledge. The wind is from the west and we are blessed with a clear night. Cezarn, you'll find some burning fuzz and tinder there. Start a small fire, make sure you shroud it well, ya ken?"

"Yes, Maleeka."

She reached into her satchel. "Here, I brought these journey cakes for tonight." She gave them two each. "You'll live off the land after tonight once your own rations run out, if you get out of there."

Cezarn pulled down his mouth covering and devoured the first one before going off to complete his task. Sooza chewed thoughtfully on his first mouthful, looking down upon the bunker.

"I'm going to set some trip threads so we can rest and think properly," Maleeka said. "Study the layout and commit to memory what you can."

She left to make the area safe even as the reality and difficulty of accomplishing their mission struck home for Sooza. He took another bite of his journey cake and sighed. Behind him he heard two small strikes of metal rod on spark stone to light the fire and then quiet again.

Will we even be able to see the stars to navigate inside there? Sooza wondered.

Standing with his back to the others, he contemplated the scale of their mission. He stood there for a while, oblivious to the movements of the others in the background. He then realized everything felt—*extra* quiet. Gripped by an inner dread, he turned to look for the others. He saw the makeshift fireplace his brother had just constructed with a gathering of stones and burning material. The beginnings of a lazy flame flickered out of the top of a small pyramid of tinder and moss, but where was Cezarn—or Maleeka, for that matter?

Sooza's breath caught as he realized that both were ominously absent. From the shadows a tall intimidating figure stepped into view and stopped at the edge of the firelight. Unconsciously, Sooza's bottom two hands reached for blades on the back of his belts.

Scarzen.

His eyes searched for Cezarn. The Scarzen suddenly blurred from sight and moved at a speed hard to comprehend. Losing sight of them, Sooza made ready to stand his ground. He wanted to send a warning whistle, but some other more potent instinct pressed him not to alert the enemy to his support. He put his back to the cliff's edge, believing an approach from that side was unlikely. Then, suddenly, the figure phased into view again, just a few steps away. The Scarzen's brazen reemergence right in front of him shook Sooza's confidence. Much closer now, Sooza recognized the warrior as one of the unit who had passed their way earlier.

The Scarzen stood there, glaring at Sooza, with that cruel double-headed axe in his right hand. Sooza hurled both blades, one at the chest and the other at the neck of his adversary. The Scarzen's empty hand glowed with a subtle aura, and as the speeding blades crossed the gap to strike, the aura expanded to form a convex shield in front of him. Both blades hit the energy shield with a dull *foomp* and fell harmlessly with a clatter to the ground.

"I expected more from your kind," the Scarzen said. "No matter. Your head will still look good on my wall."

The Scarzen began to raise his axe as Sooza reached for his long knife in the scabbard on his back. Sooza watched the Scarzen's expression turn to a twisted smile, which he had been taught well, meant—no mercy.

"Then let us dance, Kurja," Sooza said, rage for the loss of his brother filling him.

Just as he made to charge his towering foe, the Scarzen grunted as if caught by something sharp, and then his head rolled back. From behind, two Quall arms wrapped around the Scarzen's face and jaw. A third brought a long knife to bear at the front of the Scarzen's throat. The blade slashed across his neck and Sooza watched it cut deep. The Scarzen gasped and staggered forward a step and bent, revealing Maleeka on his back, her fourth hand pulling on his long ponytail aggressively. Maleeka stomped hard on the base of the Scarzen's neck and he fell face-first, hitting the ground hard raising a plume of dust.

Sooza charged forward to assist as Maleeka turned sharply to face the Scarzen's lower back. She raised her long knife high with two hands and plunged her blade deep into her enemy. Struggling with all her might, she drove the blade two-thirds in before it snapped, causing her to stagger.

The Scarzen began to convulse and writhe like a dying predator.

"The head!" Maleeka ordered. "Sooza, remove the head!"

With all his strength and the wail of a Quall's war cry, Sooza brought his blade down across the back of the Scarzen's neck just under the skull. His strike cut clean through the forked spines to meet Maleeka's cut from underneath. The head rolled free, stopping after half a turn, and the hulking body of the Scarzen finally stopped moving.

Sooza looked up at Maleeka. "Cezarn?"

"He's safe," she said. "Just bound and head-bagged in the shadows where the Scarzen scout emerged. I had to choose between assisting you or freeing him."

Sooza breathed a sigh of relief, watching as Maleeka looked at her broken long knife in the dead Scarzen's pelvis.

"Never forget," she said. "There's only two ways to truly end a Scarzen: through the hearts in the lower body, or removing the head completely." She frowned. "Looks like our weapon smith will need to provide me with a new blade. You did well for your first introduction, Hunter," she said to Sooza in a congratulatory tone. "Now let's free your brother."

Maleeka hurried toward the far side of the small clearing, with Sooza following.

"Our camp is compromised," she said. "That one was a forward scout. The others will not be far behind. It's one of those we encountered from the patrol earlier."

"Yes, I remember," Sooza said.

He followed Maleeka to a place behind some underbrush on the far side of their camp. There, they found Cezarn unmoving, facedown with a bag over his head. He'd been trussed, arms and legs behind his back like a prepared roast.

"We have to get this off him," Maleeka said. "The Kurja has used a sleep-bag. If we don't get it off quickly, he will be out for hours."

Maleeka rolled him over and cut the line that went from the bag to Cezarn's bound ankles, then pulled the bag off his head. Finally she cut away the other bindings restraining his arms. Cezarn seemed drowsy, reluctant to respond. Maleeka slapped his face. Cezarn shook his head and came to full consciousness as if waking from a deep sleep. With a hand from Sooza, he dragged himself to his feet, dusting himself off.

"Are you all right?" asked Maleeka.

"Drommal-headed Kurja almost had me choking on my journey biscuit. Did you kill him properly?" Cezarn sputtered, adjusting his mouth-covering correctly in place.

"Things could have been far worse," Maleeka said. "We are now forced to bring our timing forward. You are both going to have go on ahead by yourselves."

"What? Why?" Sooza asked.

"Because one of us has to play 'chase the rodent' with the other Kurja inbound. While I lead them away, you will have time to make your way down and infiltrate Talon East. Remember what Talaza told you about the layout. Access is via an uneven climb up the northeast corner wall. Once inside, you will find the foreign guest lodgings in a cluster of buildings set in well-manicured shrubbery in that area."

"How do you know this?" Sooza asked.

"Because it was where I had to go with Analuke a few moons ago on an earlier mission. We had to meet with Princess Nattai, a Minnima officer, just down there by the east wall. We were providing her with background on the Chou. The Celeron and Minnima clans of the far south are the only non-Scarzen race permitted to roam freely inside the bunker walls. Since we were there, Analuke and I decided to do a little exploring of our own. We wanted to see if we could find a weak entry point on that wall while there were no patrols in sight. And we did."

Maleeka reached into her travel bag and extracted a folded parchment. "Your mother drew this. I'd intended to give it to Elder Makayass, but as it happens, that wasn't possible with all the commotion."

She handed the parchment to Sooza, who opened it.

"You'll notice the entry point we found is marked here." Maleeka pointed to the position on the map.

Sooza nodded. "Pra, what will you do now?"

"The first thing I'll do is get that body out of sight, then I'll backtrack his last movements." She gestured to the decapitated Scarzen. "I'll search until I make contact, then lead them on in the other direction for as far as I can."

"This is it, then," Sooza said.

Maleeka looked at him and then at Cezarn with kind eyes. "Yes, I'm afraid it is. No matter what happens, know that I, your father, and all the clan are very proud of you, Sooza. You're a true hunter now. In fact, your mother would be so proud of both of you."

Maleeka warmly embraced both brothers. "Now go. And don't look back. The way down from here is off the right edge of the cliff—there. It is a short drop to a ledge where you will find the mouth of a tunnel. It winds its way down through the mountain. The way through has one fork. Take the left, or you'll end up in the Scarzen mines, where there are many nasty hazards."

Sooza looked at his brother. "Are you ready?"

"Ready and eager as a red bark tic to burrow through skin," Cezarn said.

***

The three parted company. Maleeka went to deal with the decapitated body. The other two moved off to complete the most difficult task they had ever been given.

Maleeka paused to watch the shadowy outlines of Sooza and Cezarn disappear over the edge of the cliff. She couldn't help but pray to Hex that he would bless and guide them on their way.

For just a moment she was sure she heard a faint laugh carry past her on the wind.

CHAPTER
11

Epilogue

What treacherous path will Sooza and Cezarn have to follow inside Talon East to accomplish their objective? How will Talaza deal with leading Cosa Clan if Elder Makayass is in fact dead, and what has truly happened to his Analuke? Who is the mysterious human, Ben Blochentackle, that Uniss and Dogg have been compelled to take under their wing? What is his true significance to their mission on Tora? What does Starlin intend to do with Elder Makayass? Is all what it seems?

Agent, your extraction for the next destination in this timeline is now being processed.

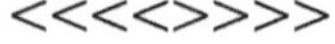

About the Author

Yuan Jur served in the Australian military as a young adult. He later sought the solitude of monastic life serving the community as an ordained Buddhist monk for many years. In Buddhism's warrior-caste arm known in the West as Zen he achieved the rank of abbot and theologian. As a theologian, Yuan Jur studied many belief systems, doctrines and ideologies from around the world. During those decades he also gained a master's degree in Chinese martial arts and medieval weaponry.

In 2007 a life threatening illness ended his monastic career and nearly his life. During recovery, Yuan Jur turned to a new venture. He combined his knowledge gained from decades of belief systems study with a love of Time Travel Paranormal alt/world fantasy as a young man. The result was a totally new immersive superverse series called Citadel 7. By 2014 his first Citadel 7 series combined trilogy had won both blue ribbon and Grand Prize in the Chanticleer Cygnus international writing Awards. He states: "There is a lot, lot more to come."